"Are you *[...]* to stay *there* *[...]*

"I thought you wanted dinner?" Mason's voice was rough.

"I changed my mind. I want *you*. Now," purred Gina, wondering at this unabashedly sexy persona she had unearthed.

It was the mask, the clothes...it was just make believe.

"You'll get no arguments from me," he said, crossing the room purposefully. Her heart clenched a little when she thought she saw his hands shake ever so slightly as he started to undo the buttons on his shirt.

He was *that* affected by her?

She sat up, sliding her legs over the side of the bed. "Let me." Though her own hands trembled, too, she quickly undid the buttons and pushed the shirt hastily over his shoulders, sitting back to enjoy what she'd only had a glimpse of the night before.

"You're gorgeous," she said against the warm skin of his stomach while she undid his slacks, only to discover he wore nothing underneath.

Oh, wow, she thought to herself.

How would she ever walk away from this perfect man...and how could she carry out her plan when she wanted him so desperately?

Blaze

Dear Reader,

This was my first experience writing with three authors where we had to link our books on a common theme—the idea of how a wrong costume can help you find your real self. Luckily, I had great writers to work with, and it was incredible fun. Halloween is also one of my favorite times of year, and I knew as soon as we were talking costumes that I wanted to write a book based on that special day.

Caught in the Act was inspired by a line from *Buffy*. As such, I enjoyed playing with the idea that no one is who they appear to be on the surface. The theme of how make-believe can bring us closer to what's real is a fantasy that Gina and Mason explore to the fullest while their lives are changing around them. I hope you enjoy their adventure.

Have a happy Halloween! Maybe don a mask or a costume that will bring you a little closer to your secret self. If you do, drop me a note and let me know through e-mail, or at my Web site or blog (you can also find me on Twitter!). I look forward to hearing from you.

Samantha Hunter

Samantha Hunter

CAUGHT IN THE ACT

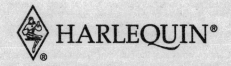

HARLEQUIN®

TORONTO • NEW YORK • LONDON
AMSTERDAM • PARIS • SYDNEY • HAMBURG
STOCKHOLM • ATHENS • TOKYO • MILAN • MADRID
PRAGUE • WARSAW • BUDAPEST • AUCKLAND

Recycling programs
for this product may
not exist in your area.

ISBN-13: 978-0-373-79502-4

CAUGHT IN THE ACT

ABOUT THE AUTHOR

Samantha Hunter lives in Syracuse, New York, where she writes full-time for Harlequin Books. When she's not plotting her next story, Sam likes to work in her garden, quilt, cook, read and spend time with her husband and their dogs. Most days you can find Sam chatting on the Harlequin Blaze boards at eHarlequin.com, or you can check out what's new, enter contests, or drop her a note at her Web site, www.samanthahunter.com.

Books by Samantha Hunter

To Karen, Tawny and Lisa—we did it!

To Natasha, Kathryn and Brenda,
for helping us do it.

Special thanks to Merri Crawford and Valerie Parv
for coming up with the great title for this book!

Special thanks also to Larissa Ione and Bryan, who
generously offered their expertise concerning Coast
Guard response to distress calls.

Prologue

JOSIE HAD TRIED EVERYTHING to get Tom the delivery guy off her mind, but nothing was working. She had to get his attention, to find out if he was really interested in her.

She searched frantically for something to put on before he showed up. There weren't many costumes left in the shop due to heavy Halloween ordering, but her eyes settled on a pleated cheerleader skirt. She grabbed the blue pom-poms and buttoned the skirt as she heard the telltale rumble of the big delivery truck arriving.

Bouncing out to the front of the shop, she watched appreciatively as Tom approached the door, wheeling in several crates of new costumes.

Yes, he was *hot,* she thought, watching how he pushed the door open with his very perfect butt. He swung around with a smile, which widened, catching her staring.

"Hey, Josie. Nice outfit. I always wonder what new costume you'll be wearing. Is it a job requirement?"

"No, I just like wearing the costumes sometimes." *Especially when you visit,* she added silently. "Kinda dorky, huh?"

His eyes slid appreciatively over her legs and the short, pleated skirt. "Not from where I'm standing."

"Oh," was all she could say, pleased enough to give a little hop and wave her pom-poms at him. They laughed.

"Should I leave these boxes here, or take them around to the back?"

"You can leave them there. I'm all alone today, so I have to check them in here."

"No boss around?"

"Just me. She's on partial bed rest. So, I'm taking a lot of hours."

"Busy season for that."

"Yeah."

She was treated to a few more minutes of watching him unload the crates and then pick up the ones by the counter. As he worked, she watched, feeling helpless as he turned to go. What now?

"Well, I guess I—"

"Oh! I completely forgot one package," she interrupted urgently. "An order that just came in this morning—can you wait a few minutes until I pack it?"

He looked apprehensive for a split second—she knew he was on a tight schedule—but then he smiled widely. "Sure, why not?"

"Great," she said, beaming at him. "I can get you a

soda from the fridge in the office if you want one, you know, for while you wait," she offered.

"That would be great. It's freakin' hot out there for October. Going to be a toasty All Hallows' Eve."

"Yeah, it's hot all right," she said under her breath, holding his gaze. "Uh, I'll be right back."

She returned with the beverage and the outgoing package—at least that part wasn't a lie. Grabbing a packing envelope for the box from the other side of the counter, she caught Tom with his eyes glued to *her* backside this time.

"That soda okay?" she asked innocently.

"Fine," he answered, not even looking apologetic for peeking. A shiver ran over her skin. The good kind. Heat flushed through her body, her fingers fumbling the job.

"Tom, I was wondering," she said softly, giving up on the task and turning to face him.

"Yes, Josie?"

"I just, uh…I mean, I wondered," she stuttered, trying to work up the nerve to ask him if he'd want to go out with her sometime. He leaned in even closer, his mouth very, very near to hers.

"What are you wondering?" he asked, and she could feel his breath against her lips. He smelled so good. Sun and sweat and fresh laundry…the uniform was crisp and clean, and her hand came up reflexively to rest on his chest.

He was going to kiss her. Her eyes fluttered shut, waiting for contact as if her life depended on it.

"Josie! What's going on? Tom?" Carol's voice had Josie flying backward, tripping over a box and nearly falling, but Tom pitched forward, as well, grabbing her forearms and saving her.

"Oh, uh, Carol, sorry...I, um," Jodie stammered again. Tom pushed his hand through thick, dark hair, looking at Carol with an apologetic smile.

"Sorry, ma'am...you caught me asking Josie out on a date."

Josie's eyes flew open. *Date?* What date? When?

"Well, listen, can you save the flirting for your private time? This is a business. I can't have customers walking in and seeing...*that.*"

Josie frowned. Carol was miserable because she was superpregnant and not getting any herself. Whatever happened to being on bed rest?

"Sorry, Carol," Josie said vaguely, looking at Tom sweetly. "Call me?"

"Absolutely."

Josie finished prepping the package and handed it to him with a sexy smile as he left. *Call me,* she mouthed and he winked.

Only when she went around to check the computer she realized her mistake. Oh, no, she'd done it again. Carol would kill her if she found out. It wasn't Josie's fault though, not completely. She'd grabbed the wrong costume from the shelf. Josie flew around the counter, hoping to catch Tom in time, but the truck was already pulling into traffic.

Then her heart sank as she remembered a bigger botch-up.

He didn't have her phone number.

1

"I MUST BE OUT OF MY MIND," Gina Thomas muttered to herself as she drove down Gulf Boulevard, shivering although it was a balmy seventy-degree Halloween night in St. Petersburg, Florida. She stopped at a light, watching a horde of children dressed in costumes and toting orange pumpkins full of candy cross in front of her, safely escorted by harried-looking adults. The light turned green and she didn't notice at first, earning a loud blast of the horn from the car behind her.

"Geez, take it easy," she said to the bright headlights glaring in the rearview mirror and hitting the gas, though she wasn't in any rush, that was for sure.

Nerves—or the fact that the outfit she had on barely covered anything—were the source of her jitters in the first place. It was like driving naked, which was nothing compared to what she was about to do.

The deep red, glittery bodysuit plunged so far up her hips and down her middle that it was more like wearing two halves of a whole suit. She'd intended for nothing to show—she'd ordered a very unspectacular ghost costume that would have covered her completely and allowed her to fade in the background.

When she'd opened the box, she'd found this instead—a scrap of shiny red with a sexy bow-tie collar, a velvet black bowler hat and cane. A pair of "do me" heels that she borrowed from her sister completed the outfit and made it a pain to drive. It was her luck that instead of a ghost costume, she'd been sent a cabaret singer outfit—a "barely there" one, at that.

It had been too late to get anything different, and her sister Tracy nearly had a meltdown when Gina tried to back out of the plan they'd hatched.

"You *have* to do this," Tracy's pleading voice echoed in her mind as Gina made her way carefully through the bustling streets of St. John's Pass toward the quiet and upscale neighborhoods of Pass-A-Grille beach. That's where she was about to crash the annual Halloween party given by attorney Mason Scott for his clients and colleagues.

Gina would have preferred to do so in a less eye-catching costume, but that turned out to be impossible. All of the local shops were picked over, and so the skimpy costume was her only choice.

Tracy was in trouble. Again.

Gina reminded herself of why she was about to do this, to keep from turning back around, going back to her comfy St. Petersburg apartment where she could slide into her favorite pair of jeans and hand out candy. She had work to do, articles to write, and she'd been in the middle of contemplating a job change. Though she'd thought about it a million times before, there was an ad for an investigative reporter position at one of the local papers.

It was a long way from her position as a restaurant critic. Gina had always fantasized about being a real reporter, getting out in the world, uncovering exciting stories. She had almost talked herself into applying when Hurricane Tracy swept in, needing yet another favor.

Technically half sisters, they'd been raised together. The difference in their paternity didn't affect their closeness, but it made all the difference in their personalities. Their parents were living the good life as retirees in Palm Springs, and Gina made efforts to see them as much as possible. Tracy showed up at holidays, and her parents never seemed to mind.

Tracy was magazine-cover beautiful, adventurous and impulsive—the exact opposite of Gina. Tracy also landed herself in hot water on a regular basis, and she came running to big sister for help whenever she did.

Gina had been covering for Tracy since she could remember. When they were younger, it was for things like Tracy sneaking in the house drunk as a skunk in the middle of the night. More recently, Gina had helped her sibling extricate herself from one bad relationship after another, including her marriage to local bad boy Rio Alvarez. Rio was in the process of divorcing her sister at this very moment.

Gina had begged Tracy not to marry Rio, but her sister never listened. In fact, it had led to one of their more painful arguments, when Tracy pointed out that Gina's dull love life hardly qualified her to hand out advice on romance. They hadn't spoken for a while after that, but they were sisters, and Gina couldn't hold a grudge forever.

Besides, Tracy was right.

Her love life was not just dull, it was dead. Gina had had one serious boyfriend in college, and then he'd taken off to focus on his career. He'd asked her to go, but she couldn't take that risk.

Casual dates and unimpressive lovers had sparsely dotted her romantic landscape ever since. When she'd taken her freelance job as a restaurant reviewer, working from home, meeting eligible or interesting men became even more difficult. Tracy, however, met enough for both of them, and apparently that hadn't stopped after she'd gotten married—or so Rio said.

He claimed that he had the pictures to prove it— pictures that would show Tracy had been unfaithful. Tracy admitted she'd had a one-night stand, and was sorry for it, but Rio had been cheating for most of their marriage. Using Tracy's single, recent indiscretion to cut her off completely hardly seemed fair. Tracy had made a mistake, obviously, and one she was going to pay dearly for.

Tracy had invested her entire savings, including college money she needed to finish her degree now, into Rio's charter boat business. Additionally, Tracy had worked with Rio for five years on the business, but everything was in his name.

Tracy could fight him, but proof of her infidelity made it harder, and the case could drag out forever, still leaving her with nothing but more legal expenses. Without the pictures, Rio's claims were weakened considerably—it was his word against hers. Tracy at least stood a chance then.

Gina did believe that Tracy had loved Rio, which made the current situation all the more difficult. Tracy had made bad decisions from time to time, her choice in men among them, but she didn't deserve this.

So here Gina was, heading to the home of Rio's divorce lawyer, Mason Scott. Their plan to steal the pictures seemed crazier as each mile passed, but it was the only option that would give Tracy any leverage.

Tracy hadn't seen the problem with the costume at all, missing the point that if Gina was breaking into someone's home office, walking around half-naked was probably not the best way to keep a low profile.

At least the odds were good that the pictures were at his home office, where Mason conducted most of his work these days, according to a newspaper article on the firm. Many local companies were saving on office space and overhead by allowing employees to work from home. If the photos were at the downtown location, which no doubt came with much better security, Gina wouldn't stand a chance.

Cars were jammed into every spot along the narrow roads of Gulf Way. It was a lovely location, overlooking the water, with a private brick boardwalk. She made her way toward the house, which had elaborate decorations and lights strung all over the porch and yard. Squeezing into a parking spot, she took a deep breath, steadying her nerves.

This was it.

Due to the nice weather, several groups of guests congregated outside. That would make it easier to blend in and crash the party. All she had to do was glom on to a group and follow them through the door. Slipping the sparkling mask that covered the upper half of her face into place, she took a deep breath and tried to ignore her doubts. Peering in the slim rearview mirror, she hardly recognized herself.

She looked...exotic. So different from her normal, understated lifestyle. She'd never met Mason Scott, although he was a familiar name in local Tampa–St. Petersburg circles, and known as a ruthless divorce attorney whose clients were never disappointed with his results. She'd also seen him mentioned in the social pages, out on the town with some notable woman or another. She wondered what he'd do when he found his pictures missing?

Second thoughts assailed her as she walked up on the porch. She nearly turned around and left after a swarthy pirate wiggled his glued-on eyebrows at her, giving her a close once-over.

What if Mason did have security? What if she was caught?

"You're late! Where have you been! I've been

calling the agency for the last hour!" A woman hissed in her ear, grabbing Gina by the arm and nearly pulling her off her feet.

"I'm sorry?"

"You were supposed to be here by seven! It's after eight!"

The woman was agitated and confused, and Gina opened her mouth to argue, but found herself pulled along again, behind a tall curtain covered in wispy netting and fake spiders that draped across the hallway.

"The band has been playing, so at least there's been music, thankfully, but everyone's expecting a singer. We *always* have a singer," the woman continued, not letting Gina get a word in edgewise. "They have your music, and everything is set to go. You go through there to the stage, okay?"

"Wait—no, I'm not who you think I am," Gina began. "I'm not the singer you hired."

"What do you mean? Did they screw up at the agency? For their prices? If you can't do this, you'll have to take it up with Mr. Scott directly, and see what he wants to do."

The frazzled older woman was dressed as a witch and more than looked the part in her agitated state. Her hat was crooked, her makeup smudged, and Gina felt bad for her. "I swear, organizing these events is going to be the death of me. Something always goes wrong. Let me go get Mr. Scott, and you can—"

"No!" Gina blurted, panicking. There was no way

she could meet face-to-face with Mason. What if he recognized a family resemblance? Rio could have mentioned her, and Gina couldn't take the chance.

Her options were limited. She could leave as soon as the woman's back was turned, but then she'd let Tracy down.

Or she could…sing.

Her voice was okay. She'd been in a few school musicals, and she sung around the house, in the shower, on karaoke nights with friends and at holiday gatherings. After a few beers, generally.

Can I do this? she thought breathlessly.

Did she have a choice? The witch was staring holes in her.

"Uh, I meant I'm not the same singer they intended to send. She was, uh, sick. So I don't know the songs she had lined up."

"Oh…" The woman put a hand to her forehead. "Okay, then. There are some with Halloween themes, and a few more modern blues numbers. If you don't know her playlist, you can tell the guys what you want, and they can probably accommodate."

Gina nodded stiffly, nerves making her so tense she felt brittle. "Can you let them know I'm sort of unprepared?"

"Sure, I'll be right back." The woman rushed off through the curtain, ostensibly to talk to the musicians.

Gina cleared her throat and tied to calm down. She'd sing a few tunes and then disappear to find Mason's office. Maybe being on stage would give her a chance to get the lay of the land and keep track of Mason. This could work, right?

Or it could be a total disaster. When the woman came back, informing her that everything was set, Gina tried to step forward, but couldn't get her feet to move. She could hardly believe it when the woman actually planted her hands on Gina's back, shuffling her toward the stage, giving her no choice in the matter.

MASON SCOTT HOPED THE HEAVY makeup and the fake fangs he'd been wearing for the last two hours—with at least four more hours to go—masked the intense boredom he was suffering. Why did he even throw these parties anymore?

Because it was expected. His law firm expected each partner to organize some social event once a year to keep in contact with their clients, old and new, and to allow for social interactions among the increasing number of people in the firm who were now telecommuting. This was the price he paid for working from home most of the time. Dozens of people, among whom it would be a challenge to find a handful he could call real friends, invaded for a few hours once a year.

His brother Ryan, a bartender at a local beach bar, walked up to him in a brightly colored Speedo. The rest of him was bare skin covered in colorful patterns drawn on with body paints.

"This is your costume? Or did you just come from work?" Mason teased.

"Hey. I bet you don't want to hear another joke about blood-sucking lawyers, but I have a couple I've been saving," Ryan threatened in good humor, raising his beer. They'd always enjoyed razzing each other about the contrast in their lifestyles, but it was all in fun. Mostly.

"Point taken."

"I thought so. Nice party."

"Same ol' same ol'."

"Where's Cynthia?"

"She went back to her ex."

"Tough break, man."

Mason shrugged. "It was never anything serious." Though the stupid vampire costume had been her idea, and now he was here stag, suffering one clichéd comment after another about fees sucking people dry, etc., etc.

Mason hadn't handled Cynthia's divorce, but he should've guessed she'd been using him to make her husband jealous—especially when their last date was at an art gallery showing that her husband managed.

Mason supposed he hadn't cared enough to…care. It wasn't as if he had any permanent plans with the woman. Permanent hadn't ever been a part of any of his relationships thus far in his life.

"You here with anyone?" he asked Ryan.

Ryan, as always, had a sparkle in his eye. "Nope, but hoping I won't go home alone."

"You never do."

"Man, you've got plenty to choose from here. How

about Little Miss Muffet over there? She's got a nice set of, uh…tuffets."

Mason couldn't help but laugh. His younger brother was an unapologetic womanizer with absolutely no interest in commitment.

"I'm happy for Cynthia," he said, meaning it.

"C'mon," Ryan groaned. "Not that again. How can you be so idealistic about marriage and relationships? You're a divorce lawyer for crying out loud."

"Hey, Mom and Dad have been together, what? Forty years this year? Plenty of people do it. It's a good thing when it works, Ryan."

"Yeah, and you see how often it doesn't. Hell, I can see how often it doesn't. Who do you think keeps our bar going but most of the divorcées in the Tampa area?"

"True. But we can't see how often it does, right? Those people never appear in my office or at your bar," Mason replied with a nod.

"Always the logical one. Should know better than to argue with you, Mason," Ryan said, chuckling.

"That's what I've always said."

"But seriously, I can't imagine settling down with one woman when there are so many beautiful ones out there."

"Someday. Someday, Ryan, maybe you'll find the one that makes you forget the rest."

Ryan grunted his doubts, leering at a sexy demon as she passed by on her way to the bar, sheathed in red spandex, her tail flicking wickedly behind her.

"Well, may that day be far, far away," he said with a low whistle.

"I'm sure it is. Is that paint permanent?" Mason asked about his brother's tribal markings.

"It's edible, man. It can be licked off."

Mason held up his hands and cut off his brother's next comment. "Okay, that comes dangerously close to an image I don't want in my head."

"Sorry." Ryan laughed, completely unabashed and not really sorry at all. Ryan's hand clamped on his brother's shoulder. "You need to loosen up, Mason. You're wearing your suit and tie even when you're not. Find a woman here and have some fun. That's what I intend to do," he said, making eye contact with Miss Muffet, who smiled coyly in their direction.

"Yeah, whatever," Mason said, feeling unaccountably old at that moment. As he watched Ryan strut across the room, he thought maybe his younger brother was right. He should be enjoying his own party, and why do that alone? Sporting a fangy smile, he started moving around the crowd, looking for a woman whom he might like to bite.

It just so happened he didn't have to look for long—in fact, she popped out in front of the entire room, appearing on the stage in a breathtaking glimmer of cherry-red. Large brown eyes took them all in for a moment, her curly dark hair framing a delicate, heart-shaped face, at least insofar as he could tell with her mask covering the top half of it.

Her lips were painted as red as her costume. He couldn't look away.

Mason walked closer to the edge of the temporary stage he'd had set up for the party's entertainment. She wasn't small, maybe just a few inches shorter than his six-foot frame, though it was hard to tell since she was wearing heels that inspired lust low in his belly.

His eyes traveled up the pale length of shapely calf and thigh to the sensuous blossom of her hip, the inviting dip into a slim waist that expanded back out again at the level of ample breasts, barely covered by slim strips of sparkling red material. She filled out that bodysuit in a way that made him stop breathing when he took a closer look. He licked his lips, wanting more than a bite.

She seemed surprised, as if she hadn't expected the crowd—was she new to this? Maybe all performers had some stage fright before a performance, similar to the nervous energy he always experienced when going to court.

Then those supple red lips revealed a perfect smile. She said "Hi, there" in a sultry voice that fantasies were made of. His dick sprang instantly hard and he was thankful for the dark outfit and the cape.

The audience crowded inward, several whistles welcoming her. Her slow walk to center stage was the stuff of all men's dreams. With a look at the band, and then back at the crowd before her, she winked. It might as well have been him standing there alone as aware as he was of anyone else—there was only her.

She was magic.

Who was this amazing woman? She ran through a little nervous patter, as if she was still getting used to the idea of being up on stage. It was utterly charming, only adding to her sex appeal. The crowd loved her before she'd even sung a note.

Mason swallowed deeply as the room went black, anticipation rising. Another light clicked on and he breathed again as he saw she was still there. A spotlight focused only on her, with her back to the crowd, revealing a rear view that was just as luscious as the front. He flexed his hands, thinking about closing his palms over that absolutely perfect ass.

She tipped her cane to a saucy angle and started tapping her foot in time with the hushed drumbeat as music started. When she turned, letting the first lyric slide out on a throaty note that was part growl, part whisper, he thought he'd died and gone to heaven, though he'd gladly follow her to hell for a body and a voice like hers.

"Man, she's smokin'," a voice said beside him, filled with sheer male appreciation and no small amount of lust. Mason just glared, drawing an inquisitive look from the guy he realized was one of the senior partners, Ron Deerfield, who was in his fifties, long married with grandchildren.

"Smokin'?"

"Yes, sir, a hottie. You know her, I take it?" Ron asked.

"No, but I'm going to," Mason said resolutely.

Ron laughed and nodded in agreement. "If I were twenty years younger and Joan wouldn't flay me alive, I'd give you a run for your money getting to her first."

Mason looked at him in shock, and Ron laughed, slapping him on the back. "Hey, I'm fifty-five, not dead. And I have the kids around constantly. They keep me young. I wonder who she is. Star quality, that one."

Mason lost track of the conversation as he realized the singer never introduced herself. Odd, especially if this is how she made her bread and butter. As she wrapped up a snazzy tune, some of the crowd sang along. She had them in the palm of her hand. People were dancing and shouting in raucous appreciation as she flipped her hat out into the crowd.

After what seemed like hours, she finished with her first set, taking bows and exiting the stage. Mason nearly plowed over a few people, including a few very lucrative clients, rushing to meet her behind the make-shift curtain. As he pushed the heavy material to the side and searched for a scarlet sparkle, there was nothing.

She was gone.

2

GINA COULDN'T ESCAPE fast enough, bolting once she got back behind the curtain, making a beeline for the bathroom she'd noticed earlier.

Lord, she was shaking like a leaf, adrenaline pounding through her system, and she thought she might be sick.

It had been one of the most incredible experiences of her life. Even if she did have a heart attack now that it was over, she'd die happy. The first song had been a bit pitchy, but then she'd found her rhythm and something had clicked. The audience was so responsive she couldn't help but let loose and give it her all. It was as if she'd turned into a completely different woman on stage.

As she passed by the mirror in the bathroom, she caught sight of her sexy outfit and flushed cheeks, and looked into her own large, bright eyes. Was that her?

Wow.

She *did* look sexy, like she'd just had a heck of a roll in the hay, though to be honest, her performance was more satisfying and exciting than any sex she'd had in her life. Sad, but true.

It had to be the outfit, the disguise. She'd once heard Halloween referred to as "Come as you aren't night," and that was certainly true in her case. She'd never been as overtly sexy as she'd been on stage. She'd never have been able to carry it off without the mask and knowing she was completely anonymous.

It was also liberating not to be compared to Tracy for once. She'd never really understood how much she craved that, to be at center stage, growing up in her pretty, younger sister's shadow. The thought sobered her and reminded her why she was here, and it wasn't for the ego boost.

She was here to steal those photos from Mason Scott, who'd been front and center for her performance. Even in his costume, she'd recognized him from his picture on the Internet Web site for his firm. He was much more imposing in person. She'd tried to avoid eye contact, but the guy was like a magnet. His presence filled the room, a sexy vampire looking at her like she was dinner. The way his eyes latched on to her made her feel even more naked than she actually was.

Oddly, she'd liked it. Or her make-believe self did, anyway.

Mason had made her hotter with a look than any other man had done with more, and she had to remind herself he was the enemy. A sinfully gorgeous enemy who had a heavy swath of dark hair falling partly down over his brow and intense green eyes. Even his makeup and fangs couldn't mask his strong jawline and passionate mouth, or his nicely shaped, classic chin.

Moving to the sink, she splashed a little cold water on her face and calmed down somewhat. Her cabaret singer self wondered what it would have been like to sing a song right to Mason, to tempt him the way he was tempting her. What would it be like to be with a man like that?

"This costume is doing things to my brain, apparently," she whispered to herself, shaking off the fantasy and intending to blend in to the crowd.

Taking a deep breath, she oriented herself in the room and spotted the main hallway that Tracy said led to the back offices. Getting there was a whole different deal—someone stopped her every three feet to praise her performance. When the waiter offered her a drink, she took it, downing the champagne in one shot and grabbing a second for courage.

By the time she reached the hallway on the other side, she was giddy and overly warm, and she had collected three men's phone numbers—not that she planned on using them, but still... Maybe she'd crash costume parties more often.

Peeking around to make sure she wasn't seen slipping away, she made her way down the hall and spotted the large double doors that led to the office. Turning the knob, she found the doors were locked, as she expected. Of course her life would never be that easy.

However, Tracy had described a second entrance, off of another hallway—one that only Mason used. Maybe it wasn't locked, since no one would be in that part of the house.

Exploring some of the pathways off the main hall, she began to get frustrated and worried—how many rooms did this place have? Finally, she saw a small door at the bottom of a set of narrow stairs, and tried that. Voila! It opened, and inside the office sprawled before her.

She might have walked onto the set of a TV legal drama, the set was so classic. Bookcases on every side, lots of leather and a huge desk dominating the center of the room. Several deep, comfortable chairs were placed by the bookshelves and there was a huge grand-father clock in one corner. She wondered if Mason was a traditional guy, or if this was just his professional persona. The way he'd watched her earlier certainly hadn't been in the least bit staid.

"Okay…so, he must have files, and the pictures would probably be in the files," she reasoned out loud, heading to several large, wooden file cabinets behind the desk.

"Well, this is a mess—he doesn't file alphabeti-cally! What the hell?" she cursed under her breath—there was definitely some kind of order to the files, but apparently it was one that only made sense to Mason. How was she supposed to search through all of these for Tracy's file without knowing how his sys-tem worked?

"Dammit!" she cursed again, unsure she was going to be able to save the day for her little sister this time.

Her search lasted only a few minutes when she

finally saw Rio's initials on a folder and she said a quick, thankful prayer.

Yes. There were several photos. Gina yanked them from the file and gasped, shocked to look closer and see her sister standing on a dock in a hot clinch with a strange man. Other pictures revealed more intimate moments, and Gina would have died of embarrassment for her sister if she weren't so angry. The pictures were incriminating and they exposed far more of Tracy than anyone should see.

But Tracy was involved in much more than a one-night stand. The dates in the lower corner of the photos indicated they had been taken in different locations over a number of weeks. Tracy wanted Gina to help her get rid of the evidence of her affair, and had clearly played on Gina's sympathies.

What should she do? Tracy was putting Gina in the middle of her divorce power play, pushing her affair with this new man in Rio's face. She just hadn't considered the consequences.

Putting the photos back, Gina decided that Tracy was going to have to pay the piper this time and take responsibility for her actions. Gina shoved the folder into the drawer. This was wrong, and she wasn't going to be part of it. They were adults now, and Gina had to draw the line somewhere.

Her relief was short-lived. It was then that heavy footsteps echoed down the hall, and she heard the dooming slide of a key into the lock of the main doors.

Pushing the drawer quietly shut, she nearly vaulted over the desk and threw herself into a large leather chair in front of it. There was no place to hide and she'd never make it out before whoever it was came in.

The main doors swung open, and Gina's thoughts raced—what would a sexy cabaret singer do if she was caught someplace she wasn't supposed to be? Instinctively, she leaned back into the chair, striking what she hoped was a sexy pose. When Mason walked in, she smiled.

"Count—what a nice surprise," she said in a sultry voice that was husky largely because her throat was closing from fear.

Mason stopped short, staring at her, his eyes narrowed. "The doors were locked. How did you get in here?"

"A lady shouldn't give away all of her secrets," she hedged, but as his eyebrow lifted and she could see he wasn't going to let the issue go, she said the only thing she could think of on the fly. "Your assistant let me in," she said, hoping against hope the woman who'd dragged her up on stage was his assistant. It seemed a reasonable deduction. She just hoped he didn't check out her story.

He nodded, and closed the doors behind him. "I'll have to speak to her about that. These are private quarters."

"Please don't be mad at her. I needed someplace to get a bit of downtime after the performance, and she said you wouldn't mind if I just hung out here for a little while. People wouldn't leave me alone for a minute."

"It's no wonder. You were very good," he murmured, then sighed. "I wish she'd told me. Then I would have known where to find you."

"Find me?" Gina said with a slight squeak, sipping the champagne she'd left on the desk. Why had he been trying to find her?

"I looked for you after your show, but you seemed to disappear."

"Oh," she said, relieved. "I was in the ladies' room."

She swung one leg back and forth, as if to soundless music, but each time she did so her thighs parted ever so slightly. His eyes fixed on the expanse of thigh she was flashing.

"Do you bite?" she asked, sliding nimbly to her feet to lean against the desk.

He walked closer, his eyes moving over her as if he could see right through her. She swallowed deeply. He was much more imposing, and sexy, close up. Trim and muscular, his jaw was square, his nose patrician. A dashing lock of hair had escaped, brushing the mask that covered intense green eyes. Then Gina made the mistake of focusing on his mouth. *Completely kissable,* she thought, unable to look away.

"You never know. Vampires aren't to be toyed with."

"Maybe I like living dangerously," she purred, almost biting her tongue at her own bravado.

Her? Live dangerously? Nothing was further from the truth. And yet here she was.

Was she actually doing this? Was she tempting this

man, seducing her sister's enemy? But he wasn't the enemy, was he? He was just a lawyer, doing his job. A handsome, sexy, successful man who looked at her as if she was delicious.

Gina wanted to think she didn't have a choice, but she was an adult and she knew there was always a choice. She could have walked right back out the door and saved her skin, hauling butt home to confront her sister. Or she could be the adventurous woman she was pretending to be, just for a while.

This was a moment that would never come again, she knew. A chance to be impulsive and wild. To be with a man who wouldn't give her a second glance otherwise. There was no denying the chemistry sizzling between them. Why not give in to it?

He had kind eyes, she thought, looking into them fully. He was even more gorgeous when he smiled. She'd come here for her sister, but maybe she'd stay for herself. Tonight, in this bad girl costume, alone with this sexy vampire, she wasn't Gina anymore. For a little while, she could be anyone—do anything—that she could imagine.

Before she lost her nerve, she grabbed the edge of his cape and tugged him down so that she could lean up and take those perfect lips in a kiss. He pulled away for a second to lose his fake fangs, and before she took another breath he was backing her against the desk, pressed up flush against her, kissing her like she was his last meal.

There was no denying his intent; his erection pressed

against her belly and she let him know what she wanted, wrapping her legs around him and pressing close, a shiver of desire spreading over her.

He set her on the edge of the hard mahogany desk, bearing down, pressing even closer.

She could feel him everywhere, but he wasn't nearly *everywhere* enough. Mason's tongue stroking hers initiated a chain reaction of fantasies about everything else she'd like him to taste. She'd had her share of fantasies, but nothing in her own past even compared. Her responses finally set her free in a way she'd never experienced.

She was so wet, her body tightening in some places and softening in others, ready for him. She wondered if it was possible to orgasm just from a kiss…it was a giddy thought, and she suspected she was almost close enough. Grinding against him, she let her head fall back as ripples of pleasure ran over her, making her sigh.

"That was very good," she said with a smile, meeting his eyes when he chuckled in response and shook his head. Had she done something wrong?

"What?" she asked, puzzled by the amusement in his gaze, though there was nothing censuring there. His hands came up, closing over her breasts, rubbing his thumbs over her to create taut peaks from her nipples until she warmed again.

"Honey, I don't know who's made you come before, but if that mere shiver is all that they gave you, you have a surprise in store," he said gruffly. Removing her top, he drew the tip of her breast into his mouth, sucking until her hands were buried in his hair, noises coming from her throat that she'd never made before.

She didn't have time to question his comment, but just wished he'd keep on doing what he was doing.

Mason ran his hands up her thighs to slide inside the strips of material that still covered her, easing both thumbs in between the plump lips of her sex. She held on to his shoulders, enjoying the play of muscles under her fingers as he massaged her intimately until she was sure her limbs had turned to jelly.

"You're so hot. Like wet satin," he said roughly, wasting no time as he stripped her of her outfit, peeling her naked like ripe fruit in his hands. "You're a siren, a singer tempting me to my doom?"

She smiled. "Does this seem like your doom?"

"Hardly," he countered. "But you are temptation made flesh."

When he reached for the mask, she turned her head away.

"No—the mask stays on," she said. "The hat, too," she said, hoping it sounded like a naughty request instead of her trying to maintain some anonymity.

"Whatever my siren wants, she gets," he said playfully.

"I want you as naked as I am," Gina responded, her everyday persona gone by the wayside as she really did become his temptress. As long as her hat and mask stayed in place, she could be anyone, do anything.

Mason shucked his pants quickly. Gina sighed in

appreciation at the sight of his large, hard shaft, fully erect.

He turned from her, reaching for something in his pants pocket. She was relieved to see him holding a small packet taken from his wallet, but shocked that she hadn't even thought about it. Normally, she was careful.

When he was sheathed, he came back and slid his hands up and down her legs before lifting a knee over each shoulder as she planted her hands behind her on the surface of the desk.

"You should know I've never taken a woman on my desk like this before," he said, nibbling the back of her knee. "But you inspire me."

Gina swallowed, her eyes catching the reflection of their erotic pose in the mirror across from the desk. "I'm happy to hear that," she whispered and met his eyes, hoping he could read in hers what she wanted.

He did. Leaning in, her ankle cradled carefully in his palm as he sank his teeth softly into her thigh, his tongue finding sensitive spots there that she never even knew she had. At the same time, his other hand found its way to her sex, gentle fingers prying apart slick folds and exploring until she was trembling from head to toe.

His butterfly touches, teasing bites and hot strokes were driving her mad. "You said there was more," she taunted.

He looked up, his smiled wicked. "Oh, there is," he promised, and increased the pressure of his strokes. She made some noise in response that barely resembled words.

"Or more like this?" he asked as he slid a finger inside of her, then two, and she lost track of everything. His hands were big, his fingers long, and she cried out as her body tightened around him, drawing him in, as if she couldn't get enough.

He captured her lips in a kiss that completed the sensual invasion, his hands continuing their work. The tiny tremor she had accepted as her orgasm was mere memory, her body reaching and craving something much more powerful, but held tautly on the edge.

She moaned a protest when he withdrew his fingers, repositioning himself and sucking her tongue into his mouth as he pressed in, his cock teasing her entrance before pushing deeper until he was completely buried, the pressure and fullness of his entry making her gasp. He withdrew, paused, then pushed forward again, their angle allowing his erection to slide over her clit every time he thrust forward.

She wanted to taste him, to be closer. She pushed upward, bringing her legs down to hitch around his waist while sliding her arms around those strong shoulders. He helped her, his own hands moving down to her backside, holding her steady as he resumed a steady rhythm of thrusts that increased in tempo as heat built between them.

Time and space blurred, her body merging with his as they tried to get closer, deeper and faster, seeking leverage that would bring them to the brink. Mason moaned deeply into the curve of her neck, swelling inside of her.

"Come with me, hon," he said into her ear, nibbling on her lobe in a way that made her cry out. Gina was rapt with the sensations of being so completely touched, inside and out, when one final glide over her sensitive skin threw her over. Her head fell back, her eyes opening in surprise then closing again as she let him carry her through wave after wave of sensation, listening to his masculine groans of pleasure as he found his own release.

Wow.

As the seconds passed and she came back to the moment, Mason pulled away. She sucked in a breath at the cool air that touched her hot skin, the sudden emptiness leaving her feeling alone and disoriented, exposed. Her world had been seriously rocked on its axis.

Was it always like this for other people? It had certainly never been this way for her, not with anyone else.

Mason took her hands and pulled her up against his massive chest, winding his arms around her as she snuggled into him. It was so sudden, so unexpected and intense, that she needed a place to gather her wits about her. Mason's warm, hard chest was as good a spot as she could imagine.

His hands ran soothingly over her back and the hard reality of where she was came back to her. He touched her gently, tenderly, like a lover, not a stranger. A stranger she'd come to steal something from. She never could have predicted how good her decision not to take those pictures would be.

"I told you there was more," he said, dropping a light kiss to her lips.

"You are a man of your word, Count," she said, trying to keep the same light tone, though her emotions were anything but.

"I don't even know your name." He smiled, as if not being able to believe for himself what they'd done. It comforted her a bit, his gentle laugh.

"I think it's better if we keep it that way," she told him truthfully.

"That's hardly fair. You know all about me." He pulled away for a moment, and she reluctantly let go.

"I only know that you are a successful lawyer, a local celebrity of sorts. On the arm of a different, gorgeous woman every week." She knew it was true, more or less. "Speaking of which, is there a date waiting for you somewhere out there?"

He frowned. "I wouldn't be here with you if there was."

"That's good to know."

"In fact, I was having an awful time until you showed up."

"Really? It looks like such a fun party," she said, though it was not her kind of thing at all. Gina much preferred a quiet dinner with friends.

"Yeah, I hate these things, but it's part of the deal. Professional obligation. I hardly know half of those people out there," he confessed, nuzzling her neck greedily. Her spine tingled, and though she'd just had— from what she could tell—the first really mind-blowing orgasm of her life, she wanted more. He could take her again, and that would be okay with her, she thought.

Just then, footsteps outside of the door, and voices with them, reminded her where they were. Had anyone been able to hear them? She laughed nervously when Mason's chin hit the brim of her hat.

"Are you okay?" he asked, detecting something changed in her.

"Just realizing how late it is, and that it's chilly. I really have to get going."

"Why? You aren't Cinderella, are you? Have to be home at midnight?"

He looked at her, his vampire makeup smudged off, probably all over her skin, his hair mussed from her hands, his sea-green eyes still warm.

"If you stay, we can go upstairs," he offered with a smile, invitations and promises unspoken. His words were sincere, and didn't make her feel uncomfortable. In truth, she'd love to spend the night with this incredible man. He was not what she expected. No ruthless arrogance or dominating attitude, he was more down-to-earth and still completely mind-blowing all at once.

"I'd really like you to stay," he repeated.

The way he said it turned her nipples hard. Sorely tempted, because what she would miss by leaving would haunt her to her grave, she nonetheless shook her head, trying to sound casual.

"I can't. I shouldn't," she responded, not sounding very convincing, even to her own ears.

His eyes darkened in a way that enthralled her. It was hard to look away, and she felt her resolve slipping. Maybe he was a bit of a vampire after all.

"You're sure you won't change your mind?" he asked in a husky tone. "I could make it worth your while."

She was pretty sure all of her internal organs had just spontaneously combusted. Though she'd just had a great orgasm, she was achingly empty inside and craved only for him to fill her again. No man had ever said things like that to her, and it was so tempting…until she remembered why she was here. That would be somewhat difficult to explain if he found out who she really was.

"I'm sure you could, believe me. I'd love to stay, but I really can't. I have to go. I have…other obligations."

He frowned. "Such as?"

"Um, you know, family stuff."

He froze. "You're married? Children?" His eyes dropped to her left hand as he pulled on his pants and she struggled to get the bodysuit on over her damp skin.

"No! Would I do this with you if I were married?"

He looked at her directly and she saw a degree of weariness in his gaze. "People do this, and worse, with families."

She thought of the pictures she'd found and admitted, sadly, that he was right. Being married was no guarantee of fidelity, though it should be.

Shame washed over her. Had she been any better? She might not be cheating on another lover, but she was certainly guilty of subterfuge. Stealing and lying, and having sex with him to throw him off the scent.

"I guess you're right," she said dispiritedly. She certainly had no room to be proud of herself, and she was still furious with Tracy.

"Hey, are you okay?" he asked, stepping close and peering at her with genuine concern in his eyes, which made her feel even worse.

"I'm fine, really." She wanted to mean it, because he was a good guy, and if it weren't for the circumstances that brought her here, this would be one of the best nights of her life. "Just tired."

"Please, if you can't stay now, come back. Spend an evening with me," he pleaded, his voice lowering, his eyes holding hers. "No promises, no strings, I just want to get to know you. Do you want that?"

She started to say no, but then reconsidered. Gina wanted that so much she wasn't sure what to say. If he knew who she really was, would he still ask?

But he didn't know. Did she dare?

What if he found her out?

"I'd like that," she heard herself say. "But only on one condition."

"Name it," he said, his eyes warm as they looked over her flushed features, landing hungrily on her mouth. She weighed her words carefully.

"We have one fantasy night. I can be anyone you want, but only for that one night," she explained, hardly believing the words were coming from her. "But we can't get to know each other. I want to be with you. To…sleep with you. But that's all."

Had she really just said that?

Never in her life had she propositioned a man for sheerly casual, anonymous sex, but this was perfect. She could let her wild side out, indulge herself and experience more of what she had tonight. She could take one night that was for her. She could be with a man she wanted, and who wanted her.

His jaw tightened. "I don't know. As much as women think men dream of anonymous sex, why the mystery?"

She shrugged. "I have my reasons. If you want me, that's the deal. We don't share each other's real lives. Just the fantasy."

He watched her closely for several minutes, and then nodded. "Okay then. Just the fantasy. Tomorrow night? Meet me here at midnight?"

She smiled, happy beyond measure that he was willing to play along.

"Midnight is perfect," she said, closing the door softly behind her and heading for her car, wondering if she'd really have the nerve to keep the date she promised.

3

MASON RAN LONGER AND HARDER along the gulf coastline than he normally did on his morning run, even
though he'd hardly slept at all. The party had gone late,
but the only person who interested him left early, after
they'd had sex on his desk.

He'd tossed and turned, dozed off, awakened hard and
frustrated. He had to wait another eighteen hours before
he could work off the sexual energy his cabaret singer had
ignited. Images of silky brown hair framing cocoa-
colored eyes hazy with passion and cherry-red lips
haunted him. She was everything he'd ever fantasized
about…lush, sensual, uninhibited.

When he got her in his bed, he didn't plan to let her
up for air until he was done. He didn't think she'd mind,
remembering how hot she was under his hands and
mouth. He could run from here to Georgia and not dim
the need to have her.

Tonight, he promised to the morning sky.

Tonight he'd have her every way imaginable, and
then they'd see what happened. Regardless of the silly

deal they'd made, he fully intended to find out who his sexy vixen was, and to see more of her. One night was just the start.

Glancing at his watch, he sighed. Sixteen hours until their midnight date. What insanity had taken hold of him that he had said midnight instead of dinner? How was he supposed to sit at his desk, thinking about what they'd done the night before and focus on work?

He needed to put Amanda on the job of tracking his mystery singer down. It would be easy enough to find out who she was through the entertainment agency where they'd found her. If she was afraid that sleeping with him could get her in trouble with the agency or hurt her career, he'd make sure that wasn't a problem.

If she wasn't married, as she said she wasn't, then he couldn't imagine why she'd be worried, except for some kind of rules that dictated entertainers shouldn't be having hot sex with their clients.

On their desks.

He could still taste her, the sweet strawberry tint of her lips, the honey of her kiss.

Sighing, he looked down and saw another boner tenting his sweatpants and started a hard run to lose it before he shocked someone on the beach.

His cell phone rang, distracting him. He slowed and dug into his pocket to retrieve it. Looking at the number, he saw Amanda's ID.

"Morning, Amanda. Great party you put together last night."

"Thanks. I love throwing your money around, but next year I hire a real party organizer."

He laughed. "You always do a great job, and I appreciate it."

"Nothing says appreciation like a big Christmas bonus," she said drily.

Amanda had been with him for years, an executive assistant he'd known from law school who'd needed a new job when she'd had to move to the area to follow her husband's work. He was thrilled to hire her and appreciated that she took on duties well past those of a normal legal secretary, like arranging his party.

"So true. Listen, do you know the name of the woman who sang last night?"

"Not offhand, no. She was a replacement for the singer they were supposed to send, so I'd have to find out."

"Can you do that?"

"Sure. But first, I need you back here."

Amanda sounded worried, and Mason frowned. "What's wrong?"

"I was checking out the guy in those pictures you had Hal take, the ones of Tracy Alvarez and her lover?"

"Yeah. What came through? Do we know the guy?"

"Not really, but I'm not sure we want to."

"What do you mean?"

"I couldn't find anything, which is odd in itself. Everyone has some kind of records somewhere. So I asked my friend Janet, down in the federal building, and she connected him to the name Peter Dupree, and then saw a Wanted file for him, for a murder in Barbados. She said that was all she could find, but suggested we turn the photos over to the FBI, pronto."

Mason cursed, and looked out at the water. "Call Ron and the local FBI office."

"Right on it."

"I'll be there soon. Thanks, Amanda."

Mason double-timed it back to the house, quickly showering, dressing and grabbing what he needed. Jumping in his black convertible, Mason made the short drive to Tampa and pulled in to the office's private lot about a half hour later. When he got upstairs, he was surprised to see Ron and Jace, two of the senior partners, and two other men with gray suits and neutral expressions whom he assumed were from the FBI offices down the street.

"Morning, Ron. Jace. I got here as quickly as I could."

"Morning, Mason. This is Agent Kelly, FBI."

"Thanks for coming," Mason said.

"So what do you have for us, counselor?" the older agent, Kelly, asked.

Mason shook the agent's hand and sat down. "I'm in the middle of a divorce case, Rio and Tracy Alvarez, and we were getting some surveillance shots of his wife and her lover—proof of adultery. Amanda, my assistant, was doing some routine background checks and became suspicious when she couldn't find anything. So she asked a contact at the federal building for help, and they turned up the name Peter Dupree, and a Wanted notice for a possible murder in Barbados, so we called you guys. That's about it," Mason said, looking at the agent. "Any chance you can tell me more?"

Special Agent Kelly let out a sigh. "We've been working with several other agencies to take down a smuggling ring. It's an ongoing task force that's been working for years to stop the movement of guns, drugs, you name it, in and out of the country."

"And this guy Peter Dupree is involved?" Ron asked.

"He might be one of their key men, but we've never had anything solid enough to grab him. No fingerprints, no witnesses. He's a ghost, changing identity, appearance, location. We've never been able to track him down, though he's left a trail of dead bodies behind him. The guy is a complete sociopath, but he's good at what he does."

"Well, I'm not sure if this actually is him, but it's what came up," Mason offered.

"You have the pictures?"

Mason nodded, having brought the entire file, and pushed it across the table.

Kelly looked over the photos, his interest intent. He took one photo out in particular and set it aside.

"The hair is a different color, and some of these shots aren't exactly focusing on his face," Kelly said.

"They were more to prove adultery on the wife's part," Mason reminded him.

"Right. But roughly, I'd say it looks like our guy. You said your client, his wife is having an affair with Dupree."

"Yes, that's Tracy."

Kelly scanned the notes. "They run a charter business? Do you think it's possible they are working with Dupree? Using the charter business as a cover?"

Mason shook his head. "Nothing in Rio's recent background or his business records, which I have reviewed very closely, would suggest that. Rio seemed as surprised by the photos as anyone. I didn't have any sense that he recognized Dupree."

"Maybe it's just the wife then, but either way, you've stumbled into a dangerous situation. You said your assistant has been doing background searches?"

Mason nodded, his stomach knotting.

"Tell her to stop. Dupree's connected, even has contacts inside law enforcement, which is how we think he manages to evade our guys a lot of the time. But if he knows you're checking him out, it puts you in danger."

"Why is he here in Tampa?"

"He might be lying low, waiting for what happened down in Barbados to blow over, but these pictures give us an edge," Kelly said, pointing to the corner of one of the photos. "This child. Sitting on the edge of the boat? He could be Dupree's son. Dupree is suspected of killing the mother and three of her relatives who tried to stop him from taking the kid. If this is the kid, then it's kidnapping."

"That poor boy," Mason said, sickened. "So you're trying to get Dupree like they did with Al Capone. They couldn't get him on his crimes, but he was arrested for tax evasion. You want to get this guy on kidnapping instead of smuggling?"

Kelly nodded. "Yeah. We weren't even sure the stories were true. There was no evidence of a child being taken until now. The kid could be our only witness. He can identify Dupree, and might be able to tell us if he killed those people. These pictures give us a big head start," Kelly said with relish.

Mason settled back in his chair, shaking his head at the enormity of it. This meant that Tracy Alvarez, at least, was involved with a killer. Mason had met Tracy once and found her a bit superficial, but somehow couldn't see her being part of murder and kidnapping. Did she even know who Dupree was?

"Why don't you pull Tracy in and ask her what she knows? She would seem to be the most direct route to the kid."

"We can't trust Tracy Alvarez. She could tip Dupree off and he'd be gone."

"She and Rio could be in danger. What if Dupree finds out about the pictures? Seems like someone should tell them," Mason said.

"If they're not involved with Dupree, the less they know, the better. Are you and your assistant the only ones who have seen these pictures?"

"Rio saw them, too."

"But he has no contact with Dupree or his ex?"

"No, not that I know of, but I don't follow him around all day."

"Tell your client there was a fire, something, and that the pictures were destroyed. Lay low for a bit. Call me immediately if there is any trouble. Is this your complete file?" Kelly asked, counting through the photos. "Negatives?"

"No negatives. The P.I. uses digital. He erases the files after he turns over hard copies."

"You're sure of that?"

"Yes."

"Okay then. If you can give us his name, we'll need to talk to him, too. We appreciate your help."

That was it. The agents started to pack up, effectively ending the meeting. Mason was a bit shell-shocked, still trying to figure out what he'd do with Rio. Their case rested on those pictures proving Tracy had been unfaithful.

"Thank you for your cooperation. Have a good day, counselors," Kelly said, and was out the door.

Mason looked through the window. "This isn't normal, Ron. Rio will be pissed, and he'll probably drop us to find another lawyer. What am I supposed to tell him?"

Ron blew out a breath, nodding. "Better than ending up dead. You did the right thing getting in here and turning it over to the feds, Mason. I say, go home, lay low until this thing blows over."

"I'll do what I can. I have depositions after lunch and a court appearance at three. I need to get going," he said, standing.

"Watch your back, Mason. Seems like you stumbled across a real psycho," Jace said.

"Yeah, well, it sounds like the feds have it under control. I hope they get him soon. Feel sorry for that little kid."

Ron nodded and the three men exchanged good-byes. Mason walked back out into the sunshine, but what had happened in this meeting still circled in his mind all the way home.

Was Rio involved? Was Tracy Alvarez unwittingly consorting with a killer? Was there more going on here than met the eye? He thought about the boy, Dupree's son. Who was looking out for him?

The brightness of the day contrasted sharply with the dark events of the past few hours. He thought of his date that evening and wondered what the next twelve would bring.

GINA WAS SO ON EDGE that she couldn't work at all, and unfortunately her deadlines were looming. She had copy due to three newspapers and one Web site on this week's "Top Picks for Special Occasions," and she hadn't been able to write a word.

She'd spent a month going to every restaurant in town, whittling down the list to the top three, and she was almost tripping over her deadline. Her editor had left three messages, her notes were all organized and spread out before her, and she sat before the blank screen, not even lifting her hands to the keyboard. And when she did, all of the writing she came up with about food sounded more like she was talking about sex.

The entrée features succulent roast pork that melts on the tongue as gently as a hot, wet kiss.

She deleted the line. Her readers weren't supposed to get horny while reading her reviews. She tried again.

The spicy appetizer bit lightly at my tongue, teasing my senses, the perfect foreplay before an orgasmic entrée.

"I'm doomed," she said to herself, deleting that line, as well. Pushing away from the computer, she took a deep, cleansing breath.

Mason was consuming her every thought. She'd relived every detail of what they'd done last night, and her thoughts were focused on what she had promised him tonight. Or what he had promised her. Or both.

Gina stood, pacing to the window, her muscles bound up tight with anxiety about confronting her sister, and about Mason. As a sensual, adult woman, she wanted to return to that house tonight so very much. As a thinking, rational woman, she knew she shouldn't. Which kind of woman was she? Which did she want to be?

She wanted to melt on Mason's tongue. She wanted to nibble her way up and down his body, enjoying every succulent inch of him.

"Great. Food and sex are apparently completely inseparable in my head today," she said to the empty room. And there was no denying that she was hungry for more of what he had offered.

She wasn't sure who she was at the moment, except a sex-obsessed dupe who believed everything her sister told her. Tracy wanted her beefcake and to eat it, too, having her illicit lover while not suffering any loss in her divorce. Gina had fallen for her innocent act lock, stock and barrel. Not anymore.

Almost as soon as she thought it, her sister burst in the door, her face eager.

"Hey. How did it go? Did you get them?" Tracy said eagerly, throwing her designer summer coat—which cost more than Gina made on a month's worth of reviews—over the back of a chair.

"No. You lied to me, Tracy—you said this was a one-night stand, but you've obviously been involved with this guy for a while. I can't get in the middle of this—you have me committing felonies now to cover your indiscretions. You'll just have to take your lumps this time."

When Tracy looked up, her eyes were swimming with tears. Gina's senses went on alert as she detected fear in her sister's expression.

"Gina, you don't understand. You have to listen—"

"I understand all too well. You wanted to get back at Rio by sticking this affair in his face, but then you realized he'd leave you high and dry in the divorce, so you trumped up a story to send me in to get the evidence."

Tracy's expression was miserable, and she didn't deny what Gina said.

"I'm sorry, Gina, but it was the only way I knew you'd go to get them. I knew you'd be mad, but I thought I could explain when you came home. I made a terrible mistake. I met Peter at a restaurant one night about three months ago, and he seemed so nice. So understanding. But he's not."

"Not what? I assume Peter is the guy you are fooling around with?"

"Yes, and he's *not* a nice guy at all. A few days ago, I was all upset, because Rio and I had a horrible fight about money—he took my name off of the checking account—and Rio said he had pictures, proof I had been unfaithful. I told Peter, because I was just so upset I had to tell someone, and he went nuts."

"Well, I can't really blame him. You've put him in the middle of this, too."

Tracy paced back and forth. "No, you don't get it. I'd never seen him like that. It was like he turned into some kind of monster. I—I thought he was going to hurt me, Gina. He even scared his little boy, Ricki, with his screaming at me. That poor kid—he's so shy anyway. He never talks. Peter doesn't let him out of his sight, though. He told me I had to get those pictures, or else."

Gina was stunned by what she was hearing. Her sister had definitely jumped from the frying pan to the fire.

"Tracy, do you ever *think?* You're in the middle of a

divorce to one jerk, and you pick up another one who sounds even worse? What is this guy hiding that he's willing to threaten you for those pictures?"

Tracy wiped the tears from her face, her eyes stormy. "Oh, that's so like you, all self-righteous and perfect, as always."

"I'm sorry if you see it that way, but you landed yourself in this mess, and to make matters worse, you lied to me to manipulate me into doing something I could have been arrested for."

"Would you have helped me if I told you the truth?"

Gina threw her hands up. "No, of course not. I would have told you to march in to see your lawyer or the police, tell them what you just told me and have this other guy arrested for threatening you!"

"I don't know what it is, but Peter is into something, something big. I see shady guys around the boat, coming and going. He never tells me about any of his friends, doesn't let me talk to Ricki much, or be alone with him. It's like he works overtime to keep an eye on everything, keep everyone separate. He was serious about getting those pictures. He said if I didn't get them, he'd go after Rio, too. I don't want that, even if Rio has been awful, he's still my husband."

"It's clear that you need to go to the police."

"No! Peter said if I did there would be consequences."

"Don't you think you're being a little overdramatic? He probably is married and just doesn't want his wife getting wind of this—he might lose his boat, or maybe custody of his son. He's just trying to scare you into doing his dirty work for him."

"Maybe. I don't know. He *does* scare me."

Gina wiped a hand over her face, afraid that her sister had really gotten in over her head this time. "Does he know where you live? That you've been staying here?"

"No, I don't think so. I always go to meet him—he doesn't leave the boat for too long. He said it was because of Ricki. He knows I have a sister, but I never told him anything specific, I swear. He's never been here."

"Thank God for small favors. You and I have different last names, so hopefully he wouldn't make a connection. Just don't go see him anymore. Cut any communication off."

"I don't think that will work. I have to get those pictures. He gave me until tomorrow, when I am supposed to see him again. And now you don't have them," she cried. "We have to try. We have to try to get them."

Gina recognized the genuine panic in Tracy's voice, and took a deep breath. If what her sister was saying was true, then there was only one way to get those pictures back. Gina took another deep breath, hardly able to believe she was even considering what she was about to say.

"Okay, here's the thing. Mason and I, uh, we kinda hooked up last night."

"What?" Tracy shrieked and her eyes went wide.

"He caught me in his office when I was looking for the pictures. I had to find some way to explain being there, and before you know it, one thing led to another."

Tracy's eyes went wide. "Wow. Well, you did look great in that costume."

"Whatever. He invited me back for a…date tonight. He doesn't know who I am, and of course I wasn't going to go."

Tracy was smart, especially when it came to her sense of self-preservation, and made the leap that Gina had already made. "But if you go, you might be able to grab the pictures! It's perfect!"

Gina had vowed to herself not to run to Tracy's rescue anymore, but she wasn't sure this was the best time for tough love, not when Tracy had an apparently dangerous man physically threatening her for the photos. If she was going to be able to look herself in the mirror, though, she couldn't sleep with Mason just to steal from him. Mata Hari she definitely was not. Maybe there were options.

"I could talk to Mason, tell him the problem. He's a smart guy, a lawyer, he might know a way to help," Gina suggested.

Tracy shook her head. "No way. He's definitely a by-the-book kind of guy. He'd probably have you arrested, even though you did sleep with him. Which I can't believe, by the way. Mason seems too uptight to have sex with anyone, though he is hunky, in his own corporate kind of way. I want details on *that*," Tracy said, distracted from her troubles for a moment.

"Forget it."

"But—"

"Listen, I'll try to get the pictures, but I'm *not* sleeping with him to do it. I'll just lead him on a little, or something, and try to get back into that office."

"Do you want to slip him something?"

"What?"

"You know, a sleeping pill or something. So you can search the place?"

Gina looked at her sister, appalled. "No! Are you crazy? I'm not going to drug the poor man."

"Believe me, Mason is far from poor."

Gina sighed heavily, sitting down and dropping her face into her hands, overwhelmed. "This is such a mess. How could you have gotten involved with a man like this?"

Tracy closed the space, surprising Gina with a tight hug. "I know. I'm sorry. I never should have dragged you into it, but I was so desperate. If we can just get these pictures to Peter, he'll leave me alone, and it'll be over."

"Okay, okay. Let's just hope I can make this work tonight."

"I'll help. I have the perfect outfit. You'll be able to take the pictures without any trouble, and he won't even notice when he sees you in this."

Gina wasn't sure how well she trusted the conspiratorial tone in her sister's voice, but what else was she supposed to do? She would distract Mason with sex, and find some way to get to the pictures. And as tempting as it was, she wouldn't go to bed with him.

She'd slip into her temptress persona one more time

for Mason Scott, all the while knowing that the fantasies they'd hoped to explore were going to have to stay unrealized.

4

THE DOOR SWUNG OPEN and Tracy nearly wept with relief. Rio came, looking handsome and serious, but all that mattered to her was that when she called, he'd come.

"Rio, thank you so much," she said, throwing herself into his arms. "I didn't know who else to call."

She knew it was wrong, but in spite of everything, she still loved him. And she was so afraid of Peter. Rio could protect her—he'd know what to do. He always did.

Rio hugged her tight, and then set her back with a suspicious look. "What are you up to, Tracy?"

"I—I'm in a bit of trouble."

"Where's Gina?"

"She's gone for the night. I can tell you, but please come in. Hurry, they might be watching."

Rio's beautiful brown eyes narrowed to slits. "Who would be watching you?"

She watched him purse his lips, waiting for her answer. Those lips had touched every inch of her, and the reminder made her shiver. She also caught the heat in his eyes when he saw her, though he'd hidden it quickly.

She'd never stopped wanting him. She'd only given in to the affair with Peter Dupree because Rio had ignored her and broken her heart. Now look at the mess she was in.

"Please, Rio, come in and I'll tell you everything."

"This is some kind of trick because of the divorce? What game are you playing?"

"I'm not. Please!" she urged, taking him by the hand and pulling him in.

Rio sighed and stepped in, the front of his massive, hard-as-rock body brushing up against her softness as he entered the house. He looked terrific in the black pants and silk shirt he was wearing. When she looked down her heart leapt.

"You still wear your wedding ring."

"Because we are still married, for now."

She wore hers, too, until Peter had asked her to take it off. At the time, she thought Peter was being romantic—that he didn't like thinking of her with another man. In truth, he was just controlling and crazy.

Rio was so different. Tracy had never appreciated that before, that for all of his faults, Rio was a gentle and passionate man. It was why women loved him. She had to hold her breath to stifle a sigh.

"What have you done, Tracy? If this is about money, we should wait for the lawyers to figure it out." His cool demeanor brought her back to reality.

Tracy turned away, nibbling her lip and searching for an explanation, but pushed him away angrily when he stepped closer.

"It's not about money."

"What then?"

"The man you saw me with—"

"Your lover," he said harshly.

Her cheeks heated, and she tipped her chin up, meeting his gaze. "At least I only strayed once," she said, her accusation hitting the mark as he lowered his gaze, acknowledging the truth of her words. "How many women did you have while we were married?"

"I think I should go," he said quietly, turning to the door, but Tracy stepped in front.

"The pictures you had taken of us… He's threatened me if I don't get them back."

Rio barked out a laugh. "You expect me to believe this? You simply want the pictures so I don't use them against you. Goodbye, Tracy."

"I do want them, but not because of the divorce. He threatened me, Rio. I can prove it. There's something else. I think it's important."

"How?"

"I didn't tell Gina, but I found this in his bedroom, hidden, the night he threatened me. I thought if I had something, you know, on him, then I'd have leverage, right?"

Rio read through several pages of the small notepad, his eyebrows rising. "You took this?"

"Yes."

"Tracy, what did you get into here? I can't be sure, but these look like times, coordinates and maybe product codes of some sort. Prices. Transaction records."

"That's what I thought, but I wasn't sure."

"This one name, here, Backman—I've heard of him. He's a local smuggler. Small-time, but dangerous."

"So that's good, right? I have something that could put Peter in jail, so he won't care about the pictures? If he threatens me, or anyone, I will use this against him," she said. "And if Gina can get the pictures, we have even more against him. He'll have to leave us alone."

Rio closed his eyes, shook his head. "No, my love. Men like your lover, they go after what they want, they take it and they usually kill whoever took it from them. You have put yourself in grave danger," he said, stepping back to look out the curtain, watching the street. "Where did you say Gina went?"

"She's at Mason's. They have kind of a…thing. She went back to his house tonight to try to get the pictures for me, but I don't know if she'll be able to do it. She's not a very good thief. I knew if I showed her the notebook, she'd make me turn it over."

"Maybe that would have been best."

"Sure. What do you care? Wouldn't having me out of the picture just make your life so much easier?"

Rio seemed surprised at her outburst. "I have never wished you harm. You know I still love you."

"How can you say that, when I obviously was never

enough for you?" she said, her cheeks burning with humiliation even while her heart raced hopefully.

Rio ran a hand over his face. "I did give in to temptation, it's true. I suppose, on some level, I never really thought you'd stay with me. That you would find someone else, something better. And you did."

"Only because I didn't have you." Tears she didn't want to shed erupted anyway.

"I've been so stupid. I know," he said. "I thought of coming to you, to apologize and try to make things right, but then I saw those pictures of you with him, and I became so angry," Rio confessed. "I only wanted to hurt you. I should have known that was how I'd made you feel over and over again."

Tracy's heart stuttered at his admission and the raw emotions radiating from his eyes. "Rio, I don't know what to think," she said softly, lifting a hand to his face, where he turned his lips into her palm and kissed the tender skin there. "But it just feels right, and safe, to be with you."

In the next moment, they were melded together from lips to hips and the world felt right again. Tracy felt solid again. Real in the way only Rio had ever made her feel.

"I've missed you, Tracy," he said roughly. "But we have to get out of here. He will come looking and when he does, you can't be here. I don't know who this man is, but he's not going to play games with you."

Tracy nodded, grabbing her coat and phone. "What will we do? What about Gina?"

Rio heaved a sigh. "We'll work something out. Call

her. Tell her not to come home. To go somewhere safe. Tell her to stay with Mason."

Tracy nodded, huddled into Rio's shoulder, his arm around her as they made their way to his car. For now, she was with Rio, and Gina was with Mason, and they were safe. They just had to make sure they all stayed that way.

THERE WAS NO TIME FOR NERVES. Gina had barely finished pushing the doorbell when Mason opened the door and wasted no time pulling her in, closing the door and flattening her against it. The length of his body held her in place as he kissed her, causing her to dissolve from the waist down.

"You look good enough to eat," Mason murmured when he finally released her lips. He was still pressed tightly against her, from chest to knee, and she blinked, bemused, not having expected such a frontal assault on her senses.

"I'm surprised you even noticed," she joked lightly, though there was no way to disguise her body's immediate response to his.

"Believe me, I noticed. Hungry?" he asked, his meaning obvious, but she also smelled something delicious.

That clinched it. She'd have to find a new job, since food and sex would be forever connected in her mind now.

"Very," she said as he leaned in, but she put a hand on his chest. "What smells so delicious?"

He grinned, stealing another quick kiss before he answered.

"Bisque, salad, fresh bread, just delivered from a place where I have an in with the chef."

"What restaurant?"

"The Glen. Do you know it?"

Gina had to bite her tongue. She knew the establishment well, had reviewed them favorably several times. Their bisque *was* as good as sex. But she couldn't divulge that, not when they needed to keep things anonymous.

"I guess we could eat first. We'll need the energy," he whispered against her lips. Then he was gone, taking her coat and allowing her to get her bearings.

"I'll choose a wine and we'll sit for a while. Get to know each other a little," he said.

He wore black casual pants and a red button-down shirt, the outfit making him look somewhat dangerous, reminiscent of his vampire self. He hung the coat in a hall closet and turned, catching her staring, and her cheeks turned pink. He didn't seem to mind her perusal as he winked and then went to go get the wine, beckoning her to join him.

"I've been thinking about you all day," he said simply, and she had no response but a smile. The words were all clogged up by lust.

As they'd agreed, Mason also wore his mask, and Gina wished she could get to know the man behind it. Sadly, that wasn't possible. In fact, sitting down to eat was a bad idea. It would lead to conversation, and the possibility for slipups. She hated to miss the bisque, but she needed to do what she came here to do, and do it quickly. Mason disappeared down the hall, presumably to the kitchen.

She caught sight of herself in the full-length mirror to the side of the door. The close-fitting black dress hugged her curves, but barely covered her breasts, which were fully featured by the black push-up bra Tracy had insisted she buy. In a fit of guilt her sister turned to fashion, sharing her most prized designer dress and shoes, and even providing a pedicure. She now sported sexy red-painted toes through the peekaboo front of the shoes.

Tracy was a tad smaller in the bust and hips, so this dress really was formfitting in those areas. Not in a bad way, but a *va-va-voom* way, Gina realized. She spent so much time in jeans and T-shirts, she had forgotten what it was like to wear something this sultry.

In the car, she'd slipped on the glittering mask she'd worn the night before, her legs seeming very long in Tracy's four-inch do-me heels.

Gina had to admit she looked pretty good, even though she'd done nothing special with her hair, letting it curl at will, like it always did. And now, her lips were ripe from Mason's kisses.

Gina wondered what it was like, for a moment, to be her sister. To live a more jet-setting lifestyle where she wore clothes like this all the time, went to clubs and parties like the one Mason had thrown and met exciting, handsome men so often she didn't think twice about it.

But for Gina, this was pure fantasy. And the problem with fantasy was that it would be a little disappointing to return to her jeans and T-shirt self. This wasn't really her, though, and she had to remember that, for both of their sakes.

In spite of his ruthless reputation, Mason was a good man, from what she could tell. She thought he might be a man she would like to get to know better, if there was any way he'd ever really be attracted to her, not her sexy make-believe persona. But while Gina did dress up for her restaurant assignments, it was usually in her standard black pants, a light shell and coat. It was her work, she wasn't supposed to look sexy.

Gina didn't even own one truly *va-va-voom* dress, and she suspected that if Mason passed her on the sidewalk in daily life, he'd never look twice.

The realization stung a little.

Still, the last thing she wanted to do was to fall for him when she was only here to deceive him. To steal from him. Gina wasn't made of that kind of stuff. She couldn't risk being here too long, because her good intentions might not be enough to keep him from giving in. Her body was already throbbing from the kisses he'd offered, and she knew those were mere appetizers, so to speak.

She knew where the pictures were, so if she could just delay Mason for a few minutes and run downstairs and get them, she'd be home free. He didn't know who she was, and he'd never know.

Hearing him whistling as he made his way back from

the wine cellar, Gina made a decision. Slipping off the ridiculously high heels so that she didn't kill herself, she ran upstairs, quickly searching for his room.

It wasn't hard to find. The door to the master bedroom was open. Candles were lit and roses punctuated and perfumed the tables on each side of a massive bed wrapped in luxurious black satin.

"Wow," she whispered to herself, eyeing the sheets. Mason did know how to set the stage for seduction.

Now she had to complete the picture.

Steeling her nerves, the dress she wore slid from her body to the hardwood floor of the hall, providing a sexy signal for him to find her, and making it available for her to grab, with her shoes, on her way back downstairs.

Guilt pinched at her, but she was doing this was for Tracy, she reminded herself.

She stripped down to the sheer black bra that showed a little too much and a black thong that covered next to nothing. Her legs were bare and tan, toned. One of her better features, but it made her feel particularly naked. How had she let Tracy talk her into this?

"You need to drive him to distraction, and this lingerie will do it," Tracy had insisted firmly.

Mason's footsteps echoed below, pausing as he called her name. She heard his foot on the first stair, which creaked. She'd noticed on her way up. He reached the top, paused again behind the door, presumably noting her dress on the floor.

Gina threw herself on to the bed, sprawling over the numerous pillows in a way she hoped was sexy just as he appeared in the doorway.

"Hot damn," he breathed out on a whoosh, his eyes raking over her as he stood transfixed with two glasses of wine shining gold in the low light. The bubbles told her it was champagne, and she licked her lips. Gina loved champagne. She could imagine licking it off of that washboard stomach of his with no trouble at all.

The way he was eyeing her confirmed that Tracy was right about the lingerie. Gina had never, ever had a man look at her like that before, with such raw hunger carved into her expression. It was…thrilling.

"Are you going to join me or do you want to stay there and watch?" she said, letting one thigh fall open as she let her fingers drift from her throat down over the space between her breasts to her belly button. She had no idea what she was doing, making it up as she went along, but he seemed to like it.

"I thought you wanted dinner?" he asked, his voice rough.

"I changed my mind. I want you. Now," she purred, simultaneously thrilled and curious where her new, sexy persona was coming from.

It was the mask, the clothes…it was just make-believe. It was all an act, right?

"You'll get no arguments from me," he said, putting the glasses down on a dresser and crossing the room purposefully.

Her heart clenched a little when she thought she saw his hands shake ever so slightly as he started to undo the buttons on his shirt.

He was *that* affected by her?

She sat up, sliding her legs over the side of the bed. "Let me," she said. Though her own hands trembled, too, she quickly undid the buttons and pushed the shirt hastily over his shoulders, sitting back to enjoy what she'd only had a glimpse of the night before.

She lightly traced the muscles of his tapered waist and the six-pack abs that she couldn't resist dipping in to kiss, touching his skin with her tongue and enjoying the vibration that worked through him when he moaned.

"You're delicious," she said against the warm skin of his stomach while she undid his slacks, the hardness beneath nudging her as she gently loosened the waist, only to discover he wore nothing underneath.

Oh my. Wetness soaked the thin strip of lace between her legs. How could she ever walk away from this perfect man? How could she carry out her plan when she wanted him so desperately?

He kicked the slacks to the side and gently pushed her back on the bed, but she knew if she felt his weight on her, his skin against hers, she'd never be able to leave. Her body ached to be filled by him again, and she had to stay in control.

Stay with the plan. Save Tracy.

Before he could cover her, she evaded him, sliding down and brushing her lips over the head of his cock, then, craving the taste of him, going deeper. He caught a sharp breath as she slid her hands around to his backside, digging her nails in slightly. The hard touch earned her an exclamation of his approval.

His hands moved from her shoulders into her hair, not forcing, but just rubbing his thumbs rhythmically over the soft skin behind her ears as she paid homage to the length of him with her mouth, exploring and taking as much of him as she could manage. She'd never enjoyed this act as much as she did right now, and had never wanted any man as much as she wanted Mason.

It was sheer torture.

He was panting harshly and murmured a warning that he was close to coming. She pulled back, smiling up at him, her hands stroking him lightly where her mouth had been just before.

"How close?"

"Close enough to warn you so you can decide how far you want to take it," he said huskily, his fingers stroking her hair, giving her control of the moment. She held her breath. She wanted to give him this, and so much more.

"How far are you willing to take it?"

"What do you mean?"

"Can you give up complete control?"

His eyes narrowed. "How so?"

She smiled wickedly, dipping down for another taste, moaning against him when his entire body clenched tight. A bead of salty dew formed at the tip of his cock and she darted her tongue out to catch it—could she? Should she bring him that complete pleasure, and then walk away? Would that make her feel better about this?

No, her conscience nagged. It didn't work that way.

She lifted up. "Let me tie you up, and when you're at my mercy, you can see how far I'm willing to go," she teased, her heart in her throat.

He paused as if considering. "What about you?"

"Believe me, this *is* my pleasure. Besides, I'll let you be the boss later," she promised with a naughty wink.

Maybe she needed to talk to someone and see if she had a multiple personality disorder, she thought randomly, because she had never been this sexy or bold in her life. Maybe she should just walk around everywhere wearing a costume. It seemed to bring out the vixen in her. But she was also hiding behind her mask, anonymous.

Mason smiled widely, lifting his arms to either side. "Okay. If that's your fantasy, then I'm in. Where do you want me?"

"Why, on the bed of course. I want to have you where I can lick every delicious inch of you at my leisure." She meant every word, and her heart ached for what she was about to do because of it. "Do you, um, have something we could use? Something to bind your wrists?"

His eyes darkened with excitement, and there was an answering response in her belly.

"I have some old neckties—in the bottom dresser drawer."

They switched places as he got on the bed and she found the ties, proceeding to attach his arms to the posts, tying his wrists firmly but not so tightly that he wouldn't be able to get free…eventually. It would give her the time she needed.

When she finished, she didn't step back, didn't think about the trust he was offering her—the trust she was abusing. Instead, she leaned in to kiss him, and found herself drawn deeper and deeper, levering herself over and sliding her sex, barely covered by the thong, over the ridge of his erection.

Bad move. She was so tempted to just rip off the scrap and take him for the ride of her life, but she couldn't, no matter how much she wanted to.

"Hey," she said, her voice husky. He probably thought it was from desire, but it was really from the tears she held back.

Never, ever again, she promised in her mind. From now on Tracy was on her own. But right then, her sister's safety was on the line.

"What?" he asked, staring at her deeply.

"You have anything downstairs, you know, like honey or chocolate sauce?"

His eyes widened. "Uh, yeah, there's some honey on the kitchen counter."

"Perfect." She pushed off him, her feet hitting the floor. "I'll be right back."

She hoped he couldn't see how she quickly dipped and picked up her dress and pulled it on over her, running down the stairs, skipping the creaking step lightly. She left her shoes there by the door. She'd get them on the way out.

Scurrying down the hall toward the office, she slid inside the room, not closing the door so that he wouldn't hear the noise.

Gina found the drawer where the pictures were the day before and opened it, searching for the envelope with Rio's name on it—it wasn't there.

"How can you not be there? What the hell?" she asked the room on an urgent whisper. "Okay, okay, think," she commanded herself, and saw a stack of files and Mason's briefcase on the chair by the desk.

Looking upward, she knew she didn't have much time before he got suspicious—she had to get the pictures and scoot. Pushing files aside she found nothing. They were gone. Peeking at the door, her breath came too quickly and she thought she might be ill.

Where could they be?

5

MASON STARTED TO CALL OUT, but it hit him that he hadn't asked her name…again. So he just yelled, hoping she would respond. It didn't take this long to get to the kitchen and back.

Something wasn't right, and as his desire diminished, his anger increased. Arousal was gone as he struggled himself out of the ties. Good thing his sexy seductress didn't know how to make a decent knot. Having Amanda find him this way in the morning would not be his first choice.

Pulling his pants on, he walked out softly, noticing the dress was gone. Had she lost her nerve? He found that hard to believe. She'd seemed really into it.

Walking down the stairs, he noticed the shoes still there, and the coat. There was a shuffling noise, like a drawer opening and closing, coming from the vicinity of his office.

Grabbing the shoes, he marched in that direction. As he guessed, the door was open, and she was so caught up in rifling through his papers, that she didn't realize he was there for several minutes. He waited, wondering if she'd find what she was looking for. Her beautiful features were quite frustrated.

Looking up to where he stood, she gasped and ran for the other door, but Mason beat her there. Her heels dangled from the fingers of his right hand as he watched her, her chest heaving heavy, panicked breaths.

Caught.

"Hey, Cinderella—you forgot your shoes," he said with no small amount of sarcasm.

She backed up another step, obviously unsure what to do. "Mason, please, I can explain."

"And I can't wait to hear it," he said, stepping inside the office and closing the two of them inside. "Let's start with your name and whom you're working for, and we'll go from there." He stared at her, hard. "So, what were you looking for?"

"What do you mean?" she bluffed, and pretty lamely.

A part of Mason wished it wasn't true, and it wasn't the part that was still aching between his legs. Well, it was, but his disappointment drove deeper, leaving a well of something bitter and dull inside his chest. He'd wanted her in bed, sure, but for some reason, he thought he'd found…what? His perfect fantasy woman?

He watched her back away until her firm butt hit the desk where they'd had their clinch the night before. She was still gorgeous. For the first time he understood how men caved to treacherous women spies who promised them anything for the secrets they kept.

Taking in the way her breasts lifted and fell as her nervous breathing pushed them higher, he was almost willing to just give her what she wanted if she'd finish what they started upstairs.

Almost, but not quite. "So, how about we lose the masks and you tell me who you are and what you're looking for."

"I, uh," she stammered, and then her shoulders slumped in defeat, her delicate hands rising to touch the back of her hair to work the clasp of the mask. When she pulled it away, there was a click in the back of his brain. Not only was she beautiful, but she also looked familiar. He'd seen her before…somewhere.

"I know you," he said vaguely, waiting for her to fill in the blank spot, distracted by the cute way her nose tipped up a little at the end and intrigued by the heat that invaded cheeks that had gone pale when she'd been caught.

"Are you a private investigator? A reporter? Or a garden variety thief?" he guessed, trying to figure out where he would have seen her. He didn't really think she was a simple burglar; there were valuables, including his computer, that she hadn't even looked at.

"Do I look like a private investigator?" she asked with more sauciness than he would have expected, given the situation.

"I could just call the police and have you arrested for breaking and entering."

"I didn't break in. You let me in," she countered defensively.

"They won't know that," he threatened, even though he had no intention of calling anyone. Not yet.

"Do you work for Peter Dupree?" he ventured to catch her reaction and, sure enough, hit a target as he saw she recognized the name.

Damn. He reached for his cell phone, and she stepped forward, speaking, finally.

"No, please don't," she said breathlessly, her voice trembling slightly, eyes watery.

"If you're in with Dupree, I want no part of it. I assume he sent you here to seduce me, so you could get the pictures?"

She drew back in surprise, as if he'd hit close to the mark again, but then shook her head.

"No, you don't understand, I'm not working for Dupree...I'm, I'm..." She took a deep breath, and he saw her hand shake as it lifted to dash away a stray tear. "I'm Gina Thomas. I'm Tracy Alvarez's sister."

Now it was his turn to be surprised.

He studied her face and nodded. That's where he had seen her, in one of the pictures that Rio had at his home. Mason had dropped by to give Rio some paperwork and saw a family picture on the table. It had been an older picture, and he never would have equated the quiet, plainly dressed woman in the photo with the dazzling, smart-mouthed seductress standing before him now.

"So you know Tracy is having an affair with Dupree. What's your role in all of this? Some kinky three-way thing?"

Her face contorted in something between disgust and anger. "No. Are you a sicko or something? No!"

"You'd better start from the beginning, Gina. I want to know what's going on. All of it."

"Okay, just listen," she said, sinking into the chair where she'd sat when he saw her the night before. Realization dawned.

"You were in here trying to find the pictures last night, and you didn't. That's why you agreed to come back."

"No, I did find them."

"Then why didn't you take them?" And why did she stick around and have sex with him on his desk? To get the invitation back, he presumed darkly. He'd fallen for it, too.

"Tracy needed me to get those photos and I agreed because…she's my little sister. She told me the affair was just a one-night stand that you and Rio were using against her. Considering how awful a husband he was, I couldn't let that happen. Then—" Gina paused, and he didn't say a word as she continued "—then I saw the pictures weren't exactly what she told me. So I put them back. I didn't take anything."

"So why did you have sex with me, and come back for more?"

Her cheeks burned dark red, and he almost felt bad for embarrassing her.

"Because I wanted it," she said, but then looked him in the eye. "I had sex with you last night because I got carried away. I enjoyed it. I was coming back because

I wanted more, to have that fantasy night with you, but I knew you couldn't find out who I was. Then, Tracy told me about Dupree, and I knew I had to try to get the pictures. But that was *after*. It wasn't why I did what I did last night."

"I wish I could believe that. Do you have any idea who Peter Dupree is?"

She shook her head. "Not specifically, but Tracy was afraid of him. He threatened her."

"Do you always agree to commit felonies for family?" he asked, drawing a sharp look from her.

"She's my sister," Gina said, as if that explained it all. "I'm sorry. I hated doing this, but I never intended to see it through—having sex—with you tonight, because I knew I was here to take the pictures."

He couldn't deny the smidge of admiration her words evoked. Would he go that far for Ryan? Probably, but his brother, while uninhibited, would never land himself in a situation that demanded it.

"Why should I believe you?"

"This guy, Peter Dupree, he's dangerous. He told Tracy that he'd hurt her if she didn't get the pictures back, or worse. She was really frightened. I couldn't let that happen."

"So you came back here to get them."

"Yes," she said with a defiant tip of her chin.

He said nothing.

She shook her head, then, her shoulders slumping.

"I wanted to help Tracy," she said, her voice choking

again. "When I knew I'd have to steal those pictures, to trick you, I hated it," she said vehemently. "Tracy is always getting herself into these messes, and she usually needs me to help her out of them. I knew she'd gone too far this time, but still…"

Mason cursed and shoved a hand into the pocket of his pants, pacing, unsure which instinct to go with. He trusted his instincts, and though it went against every ounce of common sense he had, he believed her. He wasn't going to let her know that, not yet.

"Why didn't you just go to the police, or come to me? Why not tell someone you were being threatened, that Tracy was in danger? And how do you know she's not in with this guy, and helping him out by getting the pictures?"

He saw for a moment the flash of uncertainty. It didn't occur to her that her sister might be involved with Dupree and playing her for a patsy.

"No," Gina asserted, but weakly. "He warned her about going to the police. He said he had people on the inside and he'd know. She was truly terrified. She said he even scared his little boy, who hardly speaks, and is almost kept like a captive."

Mason nodded. Agent Kelly had said much the same thing, that Dupree had feelers inside law enforcement. It wasn't surprising. Cops could be as corrupt as anyone else, he knew. It added credibility to Gina's story, but then he latched on to something else.

"Wait—she knows about the boy? His son?"

Gina shrugged. "She mentioned him. She felt bad for him. Said Peter keeps him locked up on the boat."

"Well, Dupree supposedly killed the boy's mother, and then kidnapped the kid." Mason noted the horror in her reflection. It was more confirmation that this was new to her.

"You couldn't find the pictures because I turned them over to the feds. They made it clear that anyone who knows is in danger from this guy. And it sounds like you know more than you should. So does Tracy."

"I can't believe this. I thought, at worse, that the guy was trying to hide from his wife or something. But kidnapping? His own son? Killing people? What has Tracy gotten herself into?" Gina's voice rose with each question and she stood.

"The important part is that we know Dupree knows about the photos now, from Tracy—that changes everything."

"Why?"

"The FBI agent thought we were probably safe as long as Dupree didn't know—but he does."

"Tracy said she had until tomorrow to bring him the pictures."

Mason nodded. "Okay. That buys us some time."

Gina sagged a little farther and he stepped forward, but then her back straightened, and she pulled herself up.

"Your brother-in-law and your sister are being investigated, to gather the degree of their involvement with Dupree."

"There's no way Tracy knows about this," Gina insisted, stepping forward.

"The special agents I spoke with will want to talk to you. Anything you know, you have to tell them. It could help put Tracy in the clear, and protect her, if she comes clean with them. She was right, she is in grave danger. Rio, too."

Brown eyes went wide. "You believe me?"

He hesitated before answering. "Yes, I do. Your sister has also put *you* in a great deal of danger."

She closed her eyes. "Tracy is…Tracy," she said with a shrug and a small smile. "She had no idea about Dupree. I'm sure of that. She's just always been impulsive. She's always needed attention, to be the focus, in the spotlight."

"Even if she had to get in trouble to keep it?"

"I suppose, though I never thought of it that way. She's…uninhibited. Adventurous. In many ways, I always admired that about her, because we're total opposites. We always have been."

"That's probably a good thing."

"Cut her a break," Gina said loyally. "Rio was a lousy husband, and she turned to someone who would give her what she was missing in her marriage."

"Dupree."

"Yes. She said he was handsome, sexy and he was good to her. Until she told him about the pictures."

"Well, she got attention from the wrong guy this time."

"Tracy isn't big on common sense, never has been. Most people find it charming, especially men."

Mason quirked a curious eyebrow. "So you make a practice of bailing her out? How is that supposed to help her? She never learns from her mistakes."

Gina stiffened defensively. "That might be true, but not this time. Tracy has made some bad decisions, but she doesn't deserve this."

"No, you're right."

Mason found Gina even more attractive when she had that fire in her eyes. Even more so now than he had before, which was strange, considering the circumstances. Mason valued commitment, maybe more than most people because of what he saw day in and day out. The fact that Gina was willing to do anything—almost anything—to help her troubled sister impressed him.

Who knew what Tracy Alvarez's motives or methods were, but Gina, at worst, was a sister who cared too much. That had made her an easy target, especially if Tracy was used to Gina cleaning up her messes. Mason believed Gina, but the jury was still out on Tracy as far as he was concerned.

"You said you agreed to come here for your own reasons. Because you wanted to be with me. Was that true?"

He couldn't help it. He needed to hear it again.

"Yes. I'm sorry," she looked away, embarrassed. "I… Last night was…unexpected. I'd ordered a ghost costume, figuring I could blend in, and then I found myself on stage, and then…in here, with you. You were… well—" She sputtered to a stop, and this time he did walk over to her, pulling her up close to him.

"What?"

"You…moved me. It was overwhelming. Exciting. I've never done anything like that, never dressed this way, or let a man I just met…do what we did. I never wanted anything so much as I wanted to be free to come here again and spend the night with you, but, well… now you know the truth."

Heat shot through him in response to the clearly declared truth. Mason was a lawyer to his bones, and at the end of the day nothing mattered to him as much as the truth. He could hear it in her voice, see it in her eyes. There was no subterfuge. She'd tricked him, yes, but she'd done it out of love for her sister. How could he fault her that?

She said she wanted him. He chose to believe her on that score, too. He was willing to risk being a fool for this woman, he realized. That had never happened before.

"So if none of this had ever happened, if you hadn't come back here for the pictures, then you would have spent the night with me?"

Her lips parted seductively and her eyes clouded with lust. She nodded, whispering, "Absolutely."

It was what he wanted to hear.

"We'll have to talk to the FBI in the morning. They need to know what Tracy said about the boy. Will she come with us?"

"Shouldn't we go get her and call them now?"

This was important, but no one could have predicted what was going to happen here tonight, with Gina, with her sister.

"Since Dupree doesn't expect the photos until tomorrow, I don't think this merits getting Agent Kelly out of bed in the middle of the night."

"I suppose you're right," she said.

"So we have several hours until daylight. What do you suppose we should do with them?" Mason mused, his fingers trailing lightly up and down her bare arm.

Gina's eyes went wide, and he smiled, watching her cheeks turn pink. "You still…you want to be with me?" she asked, as if the idea was incomprehensible.

To Mason, it was incomprehensible *not* to be with her. There was something happening here, something he hadn't experienced with any other woman. It was too early to tell what it was, but he was a man who trusted his gut. His instincts were telling him Gina was special.

"Absolutely."

He reached up to trace his fingers over the curve of her cheek, rubbing his thumb along her jaw. The pulse that suddenly raced at the base of her throat captured him. He bent to kiss the spot, smiling against her skin when she sighed. Her hand closed around his elbow as if to steady herself.

"I…I'd like that," she said. "There's no sense in dragging Tracy out of bed in the middle of the night, either, when we can't do anything until morning anyway. She's panicked enough."

"Exactly," he said, moving in for a kiss, finding himself intrigued with her eyes and lips, exploring her features. Now that the masks were off, he could enjoy her completely, with no secrets between them. "I've been thinking about this all day. What I wanted to do to you, how I wanted to touch you, taste you," he whispered against her ear.

"You were on my mind, too," she confessed, their eyes meeting as he lowered to his knees before her, her hands on his shoulders as she watched him curiously. "I could barely work. All I kept thinking about was… oh," she said, sucking in a breath as he pushed the bottom of the dress upward.

His hands fisted into the material as he kissed her through the scrap of lace that covered her. Pressing his mouth against her intimately, she cried out sweetly, opening to his kiss, the musky, honeyed scent of her arousal surrounding him.

After a few more moments of teasing her, tempting her to the edge, he looked up, delighted to see her dark brown eyes watching him.

"I could do a much more thorough job of this upstairs, on the bed."

"That would be nice," she said, catching her lip in her teeth in a way that made his blood race straight to his crotch.

"But this time, I think we'll skip the bondage, if

that's okay with you," he joked, smiling even wider when the pink in her cheeks deepened.

Rising, he held out his hand to her, and she wordlessly wrapped her fingers around his as they walked back up the stairs.

GINA TOOK HER TIME WASHING in Mason's shower the next morning. It was still very early, just after dawn, soft light just peeking through the crescent window over the shower.

His bathroom was heaven, especially compared to the small, utilitarian one she had at home. Several jets of water sprayed out from various, strategically placed levels of the beautifully tiled wall, washing gentle, warm water over her sensitized skin.

There was more than enough room for two in this huge shower, a hot tub on the other side of the room and music that emanated from speakers hidden where she couldn't see them. The bathroom smelled like him, his cologne, his soap, and she found herself becoming aroused again, just inhaling. She wished he was here, and thought about how he'd press her up against the cool tile with his hot body…

She took a breath, fanning her face and turning off the water.

How could she want him again, so much, so soon? They'd barely slept, but she didn't feel tired.

They'd done…everything. At least, everything she thought two people could reasonably do in one night. Each time, the passion exploded between them. Her body was obviously capable of so much more than she had previously guessed. It was a nice discovery to make.

At least with Mason. He seemed to know how to unlock her inhibitions, to open her up and make her respond like she hadn't even done in her fantasies.

What would happen now that this night was over? Mason obviously was a talented lover who had shown her things about sex, about herself, that she had never imagined. But what now?

He was gone when she'd awakened, disappointingly. He left a note, a pot of warmed coffee and some pastries. He was out for his morning run, didn't want to disturb her, and would make phone calls to set up the FBI meeting when he got back. All of that left in clear, strong, male script.

Hardly the kind of note she would have expected to be left by a man who had made love to her for the last six hours.

Grabbing thick towels from the warmer, she stepped out and was glad she at least had a change of clothes, using the contents of the bag she'd brought along after all.

Pulling on a pair of capris and a light sweater-tank, she slipped into sandals and finger-combed her hair, all it ever needed. Her one really positive asset was thick, easy hair. The humidity brought out the curls. When everything else in life was so complicated, she was thankful for wash-and-go hair.

A knock on the door made her start. She opened it,

to find Mason standing before her, looking wonderful and very serious.

"Morning, beautiful," he said, dipping in for a quick kiss. "I talked with Agent Kelly. He wants us down there pronto. They were going to send some guys, but I told him that would just freak your sister out. Instead, we'll go over to your place and get her, and head to Tampa to see the feds."

Gina nodded, feeling awkward. She'd never had a morning after like this one. Probably the best thing was to focus on the situation at hand, like Mason was. There would be time to think through the rest later, when she was alone.

Alone.

The thought left a hollow feeling in her chest, and she knew already her body would be protesting. It wanted more of Mason. *She* wanted more of Mason. But he was already turning away, answering the ring on the cell phone he pulled from his pocket.

Stuffing her doubts and self-recriminations down, she quickly packed her things and followed him out, finding her own phone and dialing the house. She had to get Tracy and settle this business about Dupree. There would be more than enough time for her to sort through her worries and regrets later.

6

TRACY HADN'T ANSWERED her phone, and Gina's had been dead from the night before. Luckily, Mason didn't mind her using his, but Tracy might not pick up calls from his phone, Gina reasoned. It was about the worst time possible for her stupid phone to have run out of juice, but Gina tried not to worry. Tracy was probably still asleep. When her sister passed out, an earthquake couldn't move her.

They took Mason's SUV, and rode in tense silence while she repeated her call. Very little was said about the previous night, the intimacy she'd shared with him evaporating in the daylight. What did she expect?

Their original deal was one night, one night to explore their fantasies, and that night was over. He'd moved on, and she had to, as well. They both had more important things to think about.

When they pulled up to the condo, Gina felt somewhat relieved, wanting to get Tracy and get downtown to talk with the FBI as soon as possible. Hopefully they could arrest Dupree on Tracy's testimony and that would be that.

But when she reached the door, she saw it partly opened, and her hands turned ice-cold in spite of the morning heat.

"Oh, no," she whispered under her breath.

"What's wrong?" Mason asked from behind, making her jump out of her skin, and it took him only a moment to see what had her standing still and stunned. Her home was wrecked. Everything was trashed, slashed open, ripped apart.

Finally, she found her voice and yelled for Tracy, but felt herself pulled backward by Mason.

"No, stop, she's not here. We have to go, and we'll call this in," he said, pulling her toward the car, but Gina broke free.

"She could be in there, she could need help," she said, running back toward the house and inside.

She went directly upstairs, and found only the same, complete wreckage, but no sign of Tracy.

"Gina, where are you?" she heard Mason shout, and he sounded wrong, somehow. She went to the stairs, and peered down.

"She's not here, Mason, I don't know what—" But Mason was running up the stairs, his phone in his hand, and he didn't stop to listen, but took her and hustled her into another room, closing the door.

"What are you doing? What's going on?"

Mason looked at her, his face dead serious. "I think Dupree's men are out front. They must have been waiting for someone to show. I called 911 and Kelly, but we have to try to protect ourselves until help comes," he said as he pushed her mother's very heavy antique colonial dresser in front of the door.

She heard a car door close, and ran to the window, watching two large men cross the street. One pulled a gun from his jacket as he got closer to the house.

"Oh, no. What could have happened to Tracy?" she said, but turned, jumping to help Mason push her bed over to the door, as well.

"This won't hold them for long, but hopefully enough to keep us alive until help gets here," Mason said, opening the closet. "Now you, in here."

Gina looked at him, frowning. "What? Why would I go in the closet?"

"If they find me in here, I can tell them I sent you out the window or something...buy you some time."

"No! I won't do that, you come in here with me, or neither of us hides," she said adamantly.

"Gina, please," he started, but she interrupted, her blood running colder as she heard footsteps on the first floor.

"No." She turned, and reached behind her desk to grab a heavy brass candlestick.

Mason shook his head, whispering, clearly agitated. "That's not going to do much against a guy with a gun."

"It might if he's not expecting it. Guys with guns don't usually expect people to fight back. They expect them to cower in closets," she whispered back.

Mason conceded the point and pulled her with him,

to one side of the door. A good spot to hit someone if they pushed their way through.

The steps came closer, and Gina tried to breathe normally, though her legs were shaking so hard she could barely stand. Where was Tracy? What had happened? Why didn't Dupree wait until today to get the pictures? A million questions crowded her mind.

The doorknob shook, and someone on the other side pushed hard on the door. She and Mason both jumped as a bullet zipped through the door, stopped by the furniture it encountered on the other side.

"I'll move into sight to distract him, you get him with that," Mason whispered, and while she didn't like it, it was the only plan they had. She nodded.

Then, the screeching of brakes out front distracted them and led to the sound of footsteps pounding back down the hall.

"What's happening?" Gina said, starting toward the window, but Mason pulled her back and slid to the floor.

"Cavalry, I hope, but we're staying put."

Shouts were followed by more popping sounds, and then sirens in the background. When the glass on the far side of the room was broken with a gunshot, Gina couldn't hold back a small scream, and Mason pulled her next to him, tight and close.

Then it all stopped.

Minutes later, more footsteps thundered up the stairs and fists pounded at the door.

"FBI, come out. Mason, Ms. Thomas…if you are

here, if you need help, please shout to let us know where you are."

"We're here," Mason shouted. "Agent Kelly, we're in here," he said, starting to push the furniture away from the door.

Gina looked out, letting Mason pull her through the small space he'd opened, and she found herself face-to-face with several intimidating-looking men, all holding guns. Movement swarmed below, on the first floor, her home taken over by chaos.

She felt herself herded forward, hurried along. The man Mason addressed as Agent Kelly moved quickly, looking them both in the eye. "Come on—we have to get you both somewhere safe. Now."

"YOU OKAY?" MASON LEANED IN and whispered as they were hustled off into a car that whisked them north.

Lulled by the motion of the car and exhausted by events, Gina had curled into the solid warmth of Mason's body and was dozing off. Dreams of his smoldering eyes as he'd watched her when she'd tied him up on the bed followed her into her sleep. Those were followed by dark images that chased them, and she jerked forward with an exclamation of fright as the car came to a stop.

"Hey, it's all right. You're okay." Mason's voice was comforting as she reoriented herself and saw that they were at an intersection in the small town of Dunedin. Wherever they were going, they had taken a circuitous route along the coastal towns, rather than going up the highways.

She'd been dozing for a while, amazingly, and shook the sleepy fog from her mind.

"Sorry, I can't believe I passed out like that," she said, and in spite of the circumstances, her heart warmed when he brushed a gentle kiss over her temple.

"You needed the rest."

He was so handsome. She even liked the small lines around the corners of his green eyes that crinkled when he smiled or was focusing intently. His face had character, as well as sheer beauty, the result of many smiles, laughter, passion. He was solid as a rock. That morning, she'd felt as if he was walking away from her, but the instant she'd needed him, he was right there.

And she was going to be locked away with him in some secret FBI safe house. She had wished their time together wouldn't be over, but this wasn't exactly what she had in mind.

They hadn't been given all of the details, but it was clear something had gone terribly wrong, and they were in more danger than they thought. The events of the morning came back to her with a shudder and his arm tightened around her.

"Any news about Tracy?" she asked.

Mason shook his head, his lips flattening into a grim line.

They drove farther up the coast and finally crossed the town line into the small village of Tarpon Springs, where Gina vaguely remembered coming once as a child for dinner with their parents. Normally, she traveled between Tampa, Orlando and Miami for her work, visiting mostly city restaurants, although she sometimes took in the occasional rural venue.

All she knew about this town was that it was home to the largest Greek-American population in the U.S., and that ocean sponges, the natural sponges found in spas and specialty stores, were the main source for the town's fishing and tourism industry. Other than that, as she looked around at the small town square they drove past, she didn't know much about the area at all.

"We're almost there," Kelly said. "You lucked out. This is one of our nicer places. Some of the safe houses can be real dives."

"Don't the other agents know where all the safe houses are? I heard someone mention something about a leak?" Mason asked.

Kelly looked at him, giving nothing away. "Some do, some don't. We change the locations, and there are a lot of them. I'm the only one who knows about this assignment. Still, it will pay to be ultracautious. Use your fake IDs, and if anything seems odd, even if you feel like it's stupid, even if you think you're just being paranoid, call me from the house phone. No cell phones."

The small street they drove down really was kind of charming. Older, single-family houses mixed in with subdivisions and town houses, many with cheerfully painted stucco exteriors in soft yellows, whites and oranges.

As they drove a bit farther, the houses were more sparsely distributed and finally they pulled into the driveway of a white cottage on the water. Gina started to get out of the car, anxious to get on with things, but Kelly stopped her.

"Wait here."

He got out, jacket and tie removed, and looked around, stretching as if he'd just recovered from a long drive, surreptitiously scoping the place out. There was nowhere for anyone to hide. Some lush, leafy plants grew around the sides of the house and down the back, but the front was open on all three sides. So they could see someone coming, she realized with a chill.

Going up the front steps and into the house, he reached for his gun before entering, which swamped the bit of optimism she'd felt when she saw the house. A few minutes later, he came to the front, smiling and waving, calling cheerfully, "You guys coming in or what?"

Mason smiled at her. "I guess that's our cue."

Gina slipped out of the car, walking beside Mason, whose hand settled protectively at the small of her back, steadying her. She stopped in place, looking at him.

"I don't have any clothes. This is all I have," she said, looking down at her outfit, the pocket on her pants ripped where she had caught it when they were pushing furniture up against her bedroom door.

Mason urged her to walk along with him again. "We have the credit card they gave us. We can buy some clothes, whatever we need, within reason, Agent Kelly said. We're vacationers renting the cottage for a week or two, if anyone asks, *Annette*," he said with a wink, using the fake name they'd assigned her. "Though as far as I'm concerned, we don't have to worry about clothes too much."

She couldn't repress a shiver of response to the sexy timbre of his voice.

"This isn't a date. We're here because someone might try to kill us, *Roger*," she said, using his pretend name. Gina had started out pretending to be a cabaret singer just to find her way into Mason's home, and now she was living a whole pretend life.

Then cold panic gripped her again, and she just stood in the middle of the lawn. "No," she said suddenly, shaking his arm off. "I can't do this. I can't just hide here while Tracy is out there, and who knows what happened."

"Gina, we have no choice. We can't help Tracy now, but these men can. We have to believe she's okay—she wasn't at the house, and that's a good sign. You can do this. I'm here, too. I won't let you deal with this alone," Mason promised, peering down into her eyes. He was making all kinds of promises she wanted to believe, but it was just the circumstances, she knew. Even so, she found herself very much wanting to believe him on another level.

"Okay, okay. Sorry."

"No need for that, but let's get inside."

In spite of the fear and worry about Tracy, she couldn't help but look forward to playing make-believe with Mason for a little while longer.

"THIS IS SO MUCH BETTER THAN I expected," Gina said, looking around the cozy, beautifully decorated rooms after the agents had made their exit.

Mason agreed. He'd feared that they'd be holed up in some smarmy hotel room with a couple of FBI agents, but apparently that only happened on television.

They were here alone; no need for agents on premises. Their situation wasn't considered that dire. No one knew where they were.

"It is nice. Not home, but nice."

Mason tried to stay upbeat, knowing Gina was worried about her sister, and with good reason. All they could do was sit tight until they got word. Mason didn't like being cut off from his life, things out of his control, but he liked the idea of being dead even less.

It was still pretty surreal to be here under federal protection. Alone with Gina, with no work and nothing to do but spend time with her. It was a difficult time, but it was also a second chance, in a way.

The reality of that morning had hit him on the drive, as she'd been peacefully dozing on his shoulder. They both could have died.

Mason had never been shot at before, and it brought everything into sharp relief. He always thought he had enough time to do everything in life that he wanted to. Didn't everyone?

When the bullets had been coming through the doors and the windows, all of the things he still wanted and had been putting off came into focus. Someone to love, a home, children.

For the moment, he wanted to provide comfort and try to make this as easy for Gina as he could. The myriad ways he could take her mind off her troubles were tempting, and he stifled the thoughts temporarily.

She stood by a paned-glass window, a tall potted palm at her side putting her in shadows while the sun shone brightly outside. "I wonder where she is," was all she said, still staring out the window. "They have to find her."

Walking up behind, he pulled her back against him, linking his arms around her waist. "You can't drive yourself crazy. Kelly assured us that he would let us know what happens, especially if they found Tracy. Until then, all we can do is wait."

She leaned into him. "I know. At home, I could do something. I could look for her, or at the very least, be there if she came back. Work, keep myself busy, *something*... Here all I can do is think about the worst. I don't even have my phone. I don't know if she tried to call. What if she tried to call me last night for help, and I didn't know?"

"She could have called 911, too. And there's no record of that, so don't jump to conclusions, okay?"

Gina nodded. "You're right. I hadn't thought of that."

"We have to trust that the cops will do their jobs and Tracy will be okay. You said yourself that she has a strong self-preservation instinct."

"That's true," she murmured.

"As for keeping busy, I think I can try to take your mind off your worries," he said with a smile, nuzzling the enticingly soft spot below her ear.

She sighed, lifting her hand to stroke his cheek, but shook her head, moving away. "How can I even pretend to enjoy myself? We can't just go along as if this is a vacation. It's not…right."

"I know. I understand. I'm worried, too. I also can't ignore that I want you, and that we're here alone. This morning, when those men were coming after us, well, we might not have walked away from that."

He saw her shudder, and closed his hands over her arms gently, rubbing up and down.

"There's nothing we can do right now. But we're here together. We have this time we might never have had, right?"

"With surveillance cameras all over the property," she reminded him primly. "Don't forget we're being watched."

"I asked about that. They're trained on the entryways and at strategic spots around the property, but not in private rooms, like the bathrooms and bedrooms."

"Oh," was all she said.

"Listen, let's get out of here. We'll get some food and some supplies, take a look around town."

She frowned. "My shoes are a mess from the wet lawn, and I really can't wear these clothes out."

"Okay, listen. You jump in the shower, and I'll use the car in the garage to run into town... Good thing they left us some kind of transport. I'll pick up some clothes for you. You can have a nap, too."

"What about you?"

"I'm okay. Lots of all-nighters in my world, and I won't crash for a while. Maybe I'll grab a few z's when I get back. Do you want to write down a list, things you want, or sizes, that kind of thing?"

He watched how she pensively bit the corner of her upper lip before fishing a notepad out of her purse. She jotted down a few things and handed him a slip of paper.

"Thanks. Well, I guess I'll go grab that shower." She turned to leave and stopped by the foot of the stairs, looking unsure. "You won't be long?"

He understood her apprehension at being left alone, even though they were safe here.

"I won't be long, promise."

She nodded with a small smile, and he was sure she had no idea how much her eyes were telling him. His heart squeezed a little in his chest as he watched her walk upstairs, those shapely hips moving in a rhythm that mesmerized him.

As he drove into town, he got an idea.

Maybe they wouldn't go out tonight. He'd pick up food, and they could cook, stay in the house, where they were out of sight. At least for now.

Mostly, he wanted Gina to himself. She seemed to come out of herself when they were in costume, when she was fantasizing. He'd said no games, but if there was ever a time when they needed to fantasize and leave reality behind, it was now.

7

GINA WALKED INTO THE ROOM, pleased to see that Mason had left two bags of clothes and sundries on the bed, some things he'd bought for himself mixed in. It was weirdly intimate, but their entire relationship so far was far from normal.

After what had happened between them thus far, it seemed stupid to sleep in separate rooms. If she were honest, maybe it wouldn't be bad to forget reality for a little while in Mason's arms. He had a point. Feeling guilty about Tracy wasn't helping the situation, so she shoved those feelings aside.

Digging into the bags, she blinked when she didn't find the jeans or sneakers she'd asked for. Instead, she pulled out a gauzy, Grecian goddess dress that fell to the knee with a deep V in the front and crossing straps on the back. It was a casual, summery dress, but exotically feminine at the same time. A small white box offered two broad gold armbands that she guessed went with the Greek theme of the dress.

Okay, so Mason had gone his own way with the shopping, it appeared.

Her eyes went wide as she pulled out a short leather skirt, as well, a soft black halter top, some shorts, a few sexy tank tops and a sassy hat. She hadn't worn a halter since high school! Searching to the bottom of the bag, she discovered some lingerie that she picked up and stared at in disbelief.

A pair of strappy sandals nestled in a second bag, along with a pair of soft pants that flared out more like a dress and some tank tops. It all looked comfortable enough, but it wasn't her usual style at all. Still, as her eyes fell over the beautiful champagne color of the goddess dress, she couldn't help but touch it again. She'd never owned anything so completely feminine.

Between that and the shorts and black halter, she figured she had a choice of being a goddess or a hooker, and couldn't smother a grin. Mason apparently liked variety. He was obviously extending their little fantasy into their stay here, and that idea took on more appeal as she checked out the clothes in the mirror.

She slipped on the leather skirt and the halter, pleasantly surprised to find that at thirty, her breasts looked good in the daring top, and the skirt seemed to downplay her hips and accent her waist. The leather was comfortable and soft. The feel of it, snug against her skin, was sensual, seductive.

There was a reward from doing those daily sit-ups that she didn't usually see in her normal clothes; no food reviewer could avoid exercise and expect to stay healthy. The fringe benefit was that the skirt fit perfectly on her ass, and she found herself blushing while staring in fascination.

Maybe Mason knew what he was doing. The outfit screamed sex, but it was comfy, too.

"What the hell?" she said to herself with a smile, putting on the sandals and heading downstairs to look for Mason. There was a spring in her step as she walked, no doubt the effect of her new sex-kitten clothes.

"Mason?"

She stopped, hearing a strange noise, and held still, listening.

Snoring.

Mason's long form was stretched out on the sofa where he was sacked out, still in his clothes from the night before, sawing wood like a champ. For some reason it made her grin. There was something so gentle and open about his face in sleep, making him sexier than ever.

A bolt of hot desire ripped down the center of her body and suddenly the idea of cuddling up close to Mason was irresistible. Competing desires to seduce him awake or take a nap battled in her mind until she simply slid down to the sofa and nestled into his side, fitting herself along the warm length of his body.

"What? Huh?" he muttered sleepily, and she stilled him with a hand on his shoulder before he got up.

"Go back to sleep. I need a nap, too."

"Mmmm," was all he said, pulling her in closer and shifting so she was cuddled into the comfy cocoon of his body.

It was mere seconds before she fell into a deep sleep; she had no idea what time it was when her eyes opened again. She was still wrapped in Mason's arms, but now he was fully awake and staring at her.

"Hey, sleepyhead," he said softly, planting a kiss on her forehead.

"Hey. How long were we out?"

He looked at his watch. "Four hours since I slept. I only intended to take a quick power nap," he said with a grin. "Guess I was more tired than I thought."

"Me, too."

"I see you found your new clothes," he commented, his eyes lingering on where her breasts pushed up beneath the material of the halter top. Her nipples pebbled in response, and warmth flowed through the rest of her as she detected the telling hardness pressing against her abdomen.

"Yes, you got creative."

"The only stores open today were some specialty shops, so I had to improvise. Besides, you're a sexy woman. You should be wearing sexy clothes," he said, his fingers toying with the material where the halter tied at the back of her neck.

Gina blushed. "I'm used to dressing more simply, I guess. Though I will admit, what you picked out is nice…different."

"Different how?"

He leaned in to nuzzle her ear, sucking in her earlobe and she gasped, the sensation from that simple kiss shooting straight to the *ohhhhh*-zone between her legs. Damn.

"I, uh, I feel more sexy, I guess. Like with my cabaret costume…when I dress differently, I can pretend I'm not my boring, everyday self."

"The outfits allow the real you to come out and play?" he asked as he licked along the shell of her ear, making her shiver.

"Maybe more that they let the real me fall to the background and I can pretend to be someone else. Act out a fantasy, you know?" she said, unsure if she was making sense under the onslaught of what he was doing to her ear and neck.

As if on automatic pilot, her hands found their way lower on his body, rubbing the erection beneath his pants.

"Mmmm…that feels nice. You taste incredible," he said, dipping in to take her lips in a quick, hard kiss that left them both panting and staring at each other, a silent request on his part being met with absolute approval on hers.

"I want you, Gina. I've wanted you since the first time I saw you on that stage, my sexy siren…."

She bit back the impulse to remind him that the woman on stage, the woman who'd seduced him in his office and who'd tied him to the bed, wasn't really her.

Gina Thomas was jeans and T-shirts, not black skirts and halter tops, but at the moment, did any of that matter? Shouldn't she just take was he was offering and enjoy it? Annette could be his sexy siren of the night.

"I want you, too," she admitted honestly. "I should let you know, though, I'm not very…experienced. I mean, I know the basics, but with everything that's happened, with the clothes, the party…you might think—"

"I don't think anything except that I love how you touch me," he said. He pulled the tie at the top of her halter to remove it, but she grabbed the string.

"Wait, not yet," she said, smiling at his bemused expression.

She stood, backing away from him as she retied the knot. She let her sexy image take over. She was Annette, not Gina. Annette had no fears, no regrets. Annette took what she wanted. Annette lived out every fantasy she could, starting right now.

Swaying back and forth slowly as she stepped back, never losing eye contact with Mason, she let the music play in her mind and closed her eyes, finding the rhythm. She forgot who she was, where she was, and everything but the man watching her intently from the sofa.

When she sang the first line of the sultry lyrics of Norah Jones's "Turn Me On," the mood of the song and the heat in his eyes drove her doubts away. She was his siren, tempting him, making him want her like he'd never wanted another woman. As much as she wanted him.

She put her soul into performing for her audience of one, slowly turning her back to him as she reached behind and undid the halter tie once more, letting it fall to the floor. It was liberating, daring. Excitement danced over her skin.

She heard him groan in appreciation as she put her heart into the second verse, shimmying the skirt down her legs and kicking away the sandals, completely nude as she turned back to him, finishing the song on a powerful note, and walking back to stand before him.

He looked up at her reverently, his eyes caressing every inch of her naked form. "That was the sexiest thing I've ever seen," he said, his tone thick with desire. "I'm almost afraid to touch you, in case this isn't real."

She smiled and reached down to run the backs of her fingers over a beard-roughened cheek. "It's real enough," she said, straddling his thighs and sitting down on his lap, taking his mouth in a hot kiss, every bit the seductress.

As heat flared between them he turned the tables and took control. His hands slid up and down her firm thighs then dipped between to stroke her wet heat until she was moaning into his mouth.

Her internal muscles coiled, her legs squeezing his hips as arousal coiled tighter, begging to be set loose, but he seemed to know how to keep her from going over the edge. His strong, warm fingers stroked back and forth, back and forth, until she was on fire. The pleasure continued to build, but never fully released, driving her insane.

"Please, Mason, make me come," she panted, breaking the kiss and reaching down to unzip his pants. He steadied her as they stood, shucking his clothes quickly and letting her take in his fully aroused, amazing body until her exploring gaze met his eyes.

"At your service, beautiful," he whispered. The sex in his tone melted her bones. Unwilling to wait, she stepped forward and reached out to stroke his cock, but he stopped her.

"No, I want to be inside you," he said roughly, catching his breath. "Let me grab a condom."

Gina didn't want to wait or to have anything between them. All she wanted was Mason, and grabbed his elbow to stop him as he turned away. "Mason, I'm on the pill…and as you know, I haven't been very sexually active…so, you know…" She let the sentence hang, feeling awkward, but hoping he wouldn't say no.

He paused, and she watched his breathing, deep and heavy. The wonderful muscles of his chest expanded and contracted as he took in what she was saying. "I've had lovers, Gina, but I'm always careful. I'm healthy, too, if that's what we need to get out of the way."

"Then what are we waiting for?" she said coyly, stepping forward.

He was there, next to her, gathering her in and kissing her until neither of them could breathe. The encompassing pleasure of his touch, his kiss, became her world, and she barely realized they'd moved back to the sofa. Mason sat fully against the back, inviting her to sit on his lap again. Gina considered falling to her knees and tasting that lovely, velvety hardness between his legs and licked her lips. He read her mind.

"Later. Now, come here," he said with just enough impatience in his voice to make her smile. She moved slowly, though it was killing her, and straddled his hips, bracing herself on the back of the sofa, raining butterfly kisses over his face. If he could tease, so could she.

"This is fun," she said with a giggle, lifting enough to slide his cock along her slick sex, but denying him entry even as he lifted up, straining, groaning.

"If you are into torturing me with pleasure until I explode, sure, it's fun," he said on a rusty chuckle, gasping as her breasts rubbed along his chest. "Enough is enough," he said decisively, taking her hips in his strong hands and lifting her and lowering her over his shaft. He pushed up slowly, filling her until she trembled with the sensation of being slowly, completely stretched and full.

"Oh, Mason… Oh, my…this is so…*ohhh.*"

"I know," he whispered, and tipped her chin until she opened her eyes and they watched each other. He cupped her buttocks and urged her to move. When his hand found its way between her legs to stroke her clit, she cried out, her nails digging into his shoulders as her orgasm claimed her, taking him with her as they flew over the hard, fast edge of release together.

It was fast. It was also mind-bendingly sweet and intense in a way she'd never experienced. It also wasn't over, she knew, giddy as Mason arched his powerful form beneath her, nearly raising her knees right off of the couch. He was buried so deep that she came a second time, finally falling limp against him.

They stayed locked together as she wrapped her arms around his strong shoulders and buried her face in his neck.

Had she actually just done a striptease for Mason and jumped him on the sofa?

Oh, yeah, she thought, grinning to herself as she hugged him and closed her eyes at the wonderful sensation of his powerful hands stroking and massaging her back.

"That is nice," she purred. "Everything is so *good.* I had no idea it could be this good," she admitted plainly.

"I bet it can be even better," he promised as she disentangled herself and tipped her forehead to his.

"I doubt anything can be better than that."

"Ah, you challenge me, woman."

Gina chuckled and kissed him, pushing thick hair back from his forehead and looking into his eyes. "If it feels any better, I'll pass out."

"You'd be surprised how much you can take under the right circumstances," he said, wiggling his eyebrows. "Next time, it will be slow and I'll take you places you can only imagine."

Gina's body tightened at the thought, her crotch turning hot and silky, her nipples pebbling against his chest. Was she turning into some kind of insatiable sex maniac? She was embarrassed about her quick reaction to him in spite of the fact that they were sitting here naked and fresh from sex.

He didn't seem to mind, reading her body's signals

correctly and murmuring his approval as he bent down to suckle at her breast, sending sharp waves of desire straight through her.

She knew then that she had no need to be embarrassed, and slid her hands to the back of his head, stroking the coarse smoothness of his hair as she held him against her.

Isn't this what they both wanted? The fantasy? Not the reality of inhibitions or doubts.

Like that first night in his office, he wanted *that* Gina. The Gina who wore sexy clothes and seduced him.

"You're so good," she admitted breathlessly. "But there are things I want to do, too, to you."

"We may never make it out of the house." He lifted his head, answering with a chuckle, but his eyes were hot and his hardness nudged the inside of her thigh. "I can't wait to see what you have in mind."

She leaned down to kiss him deeply, while reaching back to stroke the head of his erection, licking her lips in anticipation of tasting him this time.

"Looks like you won't have to."

MASON RELAXED AS HE WORKED at the counter, Gina sitting close by. Staying in had been a great idea. Buying the new, daring clothes had been inspired, he thought to himself with a grin. He'd remember that striptease for the rest of his life, and wondered if he could get a repeat performance.

Gina was a sexy woman, though she didn't believe it, and when she sang, his heart stopped. Still, he could imagine hanging around with her in faded jeans and T-shirts, reading or working together through a lazy afternoon, sort of like what they were doing now.

Whoa.

The little domestic fantasy had risen in his imagination far too easily considering he'd only known her for a few days. Still, hadn't his father told him that he'd known his mother was "the one" within fifteen minutes of meeting her? Though Mom had made Dad wait two years before she married him.

"What are you smiling at?" Gina asked.

"Oh, just thinking about my parents. My dad said it was love at first sight."

"Do you believe that?"

"I don't know. Maybe. I know when he looks at her, still, it's like his whole face lights up."

"That's so sweet," Gina said, smiling, too, freshly dressed in denim shorts and a white tank top that fit her well, particularly over pert breasts that needed no bra.

He met her eyes, and something lit up inside of him. He wondered if he had the same look his father did when his mother walked into a room?

The thought flattened him, and he lost track of everything. He recovered quickly, chuckling.

"I guess I should be worried, making dinner for a food critic?" Mason asked, the aroma of garlic and olive oil filling the kitchen as they used groceries he'd bought to make dinner instead of going out. By the time they had finished seducing each other into exhaustion, it was too late, and they were too hungry to wait for nourishment.

"I don't think you have any need to worry. If your cooking isn't great, you have other considerable talents to make up for it," she teased, her eyes sparkling as she drained and sliced roasted red peppers.

Her hands moved nimbly, he noted, as she cut the peppers quickly into even slices.

"Good to know. Tell me about what you do," he said, curious to know everything about Gina that he could. "I don't think I have ever known a food critic before. How do you end up in that kind of work?"

"Well, I didn't really think I would, not at first. I didn't know what I wanted to do, but I liked food, and thought it would be fun to work in a restaurant, so after two years of college, I applied to cooking school," she explained.

He interrupted, "That explains how good you are with that knife."

She smiled. "Yeah, but not good enough to compete with the best. It's so competitive, I just didn't have the ruthless ambition I needed to be a top chef."

"So it's just like on the TV shows?" Mason asked with a grin.

"Worse. It's really cutthroat, no pun intended, and the kitchens can be really unpleasant places, depending on where you end up. I didn't have the stomach for it," she said, and they both groaned at her inadvertent pun.

"So, I switched out and finished college, got a degree

in journalism. I ended up working for a local newspaper, which was okay, but mostly low-end, boring kind of stuff. Not much upward movement."

"And so you put those two together, the food and the journalism?" he said, pouring two glasses of red wine.

"Yes, though not on purpose, it just sort of happened. I ended up freelancing various projects and writing for some local food magazines, columns, interviewed restaurant owners, and it evolved into my small syndicated column, 'Spice of Life.' It does well enough that I was able to quit the paper and work freelance."

His eyebrows lifted in recognition. "Hey, I've read that column! I didn't make the connection. It's a good column. Fun, informative. I've taken several of your recommendations."

"Thanks. I like it, though it's not a very glamorous profession."

"What do you mean? You're a local celebrity, of sorts. You go to all the new restaurants, all the events. They quake in their shoes when they see you walk in."

That made her laugh out loud, and she shook her head.

"Hardly. There are food critics with that kind of power, but I'm not one of them. I try to be friendly and positive in my reviews, anyway. I tell the truth, but I know from the inside how hard these people work, and I'm not out there to tear them down."

"Admirable."

She shrugged. "I like it, and I've made some friends.

Working on your own severely limits your social life. I usually end up going to all of those events alone, and then going home and sitting up all night trying to find something clever to say about it."

"Why do you go alone? You can't take dates? Friends?"

"My social life dimmed considerably after I started freelancing, but also, when I go, I have to pay attention to everything from the service to the surroundings, as well as the food. I'm usually taking notes and so forth, so it's distracting if I go with someone."

"Huh. Okay, what would you say about this?" he asked, blowing on a spoon of red sauce and lifting it to her lips. She tasted and swallowed, closing her eyes as she did so. Her cheeks were rosy from the heat in the kitchen, her hair a little mussed from the afternoon of sex, her full lips still showing evidence of his kisses. Mason wished he had a camera.

"Piquant without being too acidic, it's an improvisational sauce that shows the cook knows how to tease the taste buds while not overwhelming them," she said smartly. Then caught her breath when he leaned in and kissed her deeply, his hand on the back of her head as his mouth explored hers for a few hot moments before he released her and went back to the stove.

He smiled to himself, stirring the sauce and waiting while she caught her breath. He turned to see her taking a sip of wine.

"And the service?" he asked.

"Aggressive, creative and unparalleled," she said,

watching him and not bothering to hide the lust in her eyes as she went back to making their bruschetta. "Also worth noting, the cook has a fantastic ass."

He grinned, putting the cover on the sauce. "I think that could be considered sexual harassment."

"Okay," she said agreeably. "Here, you take a bite. You must be hungry after all of that exertion earlier," she said, spooning a mix of vegetables, cheese and olive oil onto a freshly toasted slice of baguette.

He was starving, but she was so beautiful that the food took a distant second place to the thought of taking Gina again, right here in the kitchen, before they could get to dinner.

She was a lot of fun to be around, creative and daring, and obviously a skilled cook. As he sank his teeth into the hors d'oeuvre, his eyes rolled back and lust for Gina and lust for the food she had fed him mingled as the succulent mixture she'd concocted completely took over his senses.

"Good?" she asked, and he nodded enthusiastically, taking another bite, gently nipping the ends of her fingers this time as she yanked them away.

"Hey! Watch it," she exclaimed.

"What?" he asked innocently. "You aren't part of the appetizer?"

She laughed as he continued to lick and nip at her fingers, his arms sliding around her and making sure she didn't fall backward.

Mason hadn't laughed this freely or had this much fun in a long time. Inevitably, the playful nibbling of her garlicky fingers led him to her lips, still a little spicy from the sauce. Laughter gave way to sighs and moans as heat rose in the kitchen, and not from the cooking.

"You're delicious," he said, his hands moving up under her halter again.

"I think your sauce is burning," she said breathlessly as he ran his thumbs over her nipples.

"Who needs food?" he said. He knew she was hungry for more than dinner, just as he was.

"I do. You're wearing me out. Go turn it down before we have a kitchen fire," she said, pushing him away with a chuckle.

"Fine. First food, then sex, you vixen. And this is not all me. You're a wild woman."

She laughed again, shaking her head. "Only with you," she said softly, taking the plate from him, a slight edge of doubt replacing the teasing light that was in her eyes.

"I like that idea. You're all mine," he said spontaneously, but he meant it. They both seemed surprised, the words hanging between them before they broke the look and carried their plates to the table.

"Listen, I know it's only been a few days, but it's like what would normally take weeks in real life has been condensed for us, if that makes any sense," he said, shaking his head. "Whatever is happening between us, it's intense," he added with a half smile, digging in to his food.

"I know what you mean. I feel it, too. It's the intensity of the situation. We're here, we're forced to only depend on each other, to only be with each other…it makes it harder to know what's real and what's not."

Mason frowned. "No, I know what's real. I know whatever we have, it's special. I've felt that from the first time I touched you. I've never felt that with anyone else."

"Mason, I've been around the newspapers for some time, including the social pages. Some of your previous relationships have been with some pretty high-profile women. Glamorous, exciting. Believe me, that's not me. Tracy, maybe, but not me." She waved her hands around. "Believe me, this whole situation, the adventure, the clothes, it's the exception in my life. You even picked out these outfits, not me."

"And you look spectacular in them. Besides, it's not entirely true that I date socialites all the time. One or two, sure, but my daily life is mostly work, family. Normal stuff. Just like you. Most of the women I've dated are usually professionals I meet through work."

"But no one special? Ever come close? You know, to getting married yourself?"

"Nope. Not yet." He looked at her deeply, and thought he saw her hand tremble slightly as she reached for her wine.

"I've never met anyone I was that serious about, either. Certainly no one with whom I've had chemistry like ours," she admitted.

"I think we have a little more than sex going on here, Gina."

"How could we? Relationships take time, this is…a fantasy. An adventure."

He knew she was right, at least in part. How many divorce cases had he handled with people who'd jumped into marriage too quickly, who didn't wait to make sure it was right?

"I'm not saying we should run off and elope, but don't you think we might have something worth exploring?" He thought of his father's story, and wondered if history wasn't repeating itself.

She closed her eyes, took a sip of wine and met his gaze squarely. "I don't know what to think. This is all very exciting, but it's not real life."

"Real life can be exiting, too."

She shrugged and didn't say anything, paying attention to her food.

Gina intrigued him. She was clearly adventurous, sexually and otherwise, and yet she didn't seem to see that about herself. She was smart, sexy, accomplished and had her head on straight, but seemed to think her sister's socialite lifestyle was more attractive to him than her own more low-key one.

When this situation was resolved he planned to get to know her better, and show her how exciting ordinary life could be.

8

TRACY AND RIO PUSHED THROUGH the light brush of the plant life on Caledesi Island.

"You remember where this spot is?" Rio asked, sounding doubtful.

"Yes, it's just ahead. Gina and I used to row out here all the time when we were teenagers. We used to play 'pirate king' here with our friends during the summers. We'd hide all kinds of things all over the island, supposed to be buried treasure, in different places, then we'd see if we could find it. No one will find it there," Tracy assured Rio, running her hands over the goose bumps that appeared on her skin even with the warm sun shining down.

"Good. Let's hurry. We need to do this, and then get on our way," Rio said, stroking a hand down her hair, and she smiled at him, excitement and love swelling inside of her.

They were meant to be. All of these horrible things had happened so that she and Rio would be back together, Tracy just knew it. They'd put the meeting log in a safe box, after they made two copies. One that she'd left with her lawyer, only to be opened if something happened to her, and one that they had with them, about to hide it where no one would ever find it.

"Maybe we shouldn't call him, Rio. He's going to be very angry. I think we should just leave."

"He has to know that we sent a copy to someone who will know how to use it if anything happens to us, and that we hid the original where only we could find it. It's the only way he might back off. We'll let him know we'll never say a word, as long as he leaves us and our families alone."

She nodded. "I'm sorry I ever doubted you, Rio. And I—I...I'm so sorry about Peter, and what I did...getting us all into this mess, but mostly, I'm so ashamed of what I did with him, that I cheated—"

Rio sighed heavily, wiping away tears from her face, and his understanding almost made her feel more ashamed. It would have been easier, in some ways, if he were still angry with her.

"We all make mistakes, my love. I know I pushed you into the arms of another man. It makes me want to kill him, to think of him touching you," he said roughly.

"We can start fresh now. I love you, Rio."

His features softened, so handsome, she thought. How could she have ever wanted anyone else?

"The future is in front of us. All we have to do is finish this and leave. We can come back once he has moved on."

Tracy nodded, wondering how she could have ever doubted him. They stopped, their touches mingling, followed by kisses that deepened and got hotter. Even the humid air of the island felt cool to her skin as Rio's hands closed over her breasts, touching her in ways that made her forget everything.

"I thought you said we had to hurry," she said, unbuckling his pants, and releasing him into her palm.

"We will hurry," he said with a wicked grin. He turned her around and lifted the edge of her sundress, ripping the soft silk of her thong as he found his way unerringly to the center of her heat, drawing a strangled cry from her lips as she tried to be quiet. It was nearly impossible, as his touch and the way he moved inside her made her want to scream with how good it all was.

His pace increased, thrusting hard as he murmured endearments and encouragements, his hands making magic everywhere he touched. She planted her hands forward, against the trunk of a large tree, giving herself over in a way she hadn't felt since they had first met.

"You're mine, Tracy, and I'm yours," he said huskily, moving inside of her with sensual, perfect rhythm. "There will never be anyone else ever again."

"Yes, yes," she agreed on an exclamation emphasized by the emotions that flooded her at the same time her climax stole her breath. Rio's followed quickly as all words were forgotten.

Minutes later, they fixed their clothes and put themselves back together, making their way through the woods again. Rio lifted her hand, wrapped in his, to his lips.

"I can hardly wait to have you to myself and show you how much I have missed you. Slowly and thoroughly," he said with such erotic promise that she shivered in the heat of midday.

"I want that, too."

They found the old shack, still abandoned, and hid the copy of Dupree's meeting log underneath some old floorboards.

"Let's get to the boat and we'll make the call."

She nodded, feeling more secure. They could do this. It was a good plan. Tracy only wished she'd had a chance to talk with Gina, to let her know. It scared her that her sister had not answered her phone or returned her calls, but Rio convinced her that Gina was probably involved with Mason. Hopefully her sister would find a way to forgive her, and Tracy promised she would make it up to her later.

"Okay, let's go," she said with more confidence than she felt, and they got in the car, heading back.

MASON HADN'T BEEN OUT ON his boat in a while. He recognized how much he missed it, looking out over the water at the distant coastline, as the large tour boat they were on made its way over the waves. The water in the gulf was getting rougher as they got into winter, but he watched Gina, who stood solidly on deck, enjoying the view as much as he was. The choppiness didn't seem to bother her, either.

"I'm glad we decided to get out of the house and do

this," he said, wrapping his arm around her as they both glanced out over the rail.

"Me, too. I love being on the water. It makes me feel…free."

"I know. Do you have a boat?"

"No, not of my own. But my stepdad loves to sail and fish, and he had us on boats since I can remember."

Which explained her sea-hardiness.

"I still sail with my dad from time to time, but I haven't been on my own boat since August. Work takes over."

"Sail or motor?"

"A twenty-eight-foot sailboat. I bought it used, and usually work on it over the winter. I'll have to find time this year."

"You and my stepdad would get along great. He loves working on boats."

They entered a channel, and a man came out on deck, dressed in an old-time diving suit with a helmet, perfectly round with multiple round windows that made him look as if he'd come out of an old movie.

"What's he doing?" Gina wondered out loud.

"I think he's going to dive for sponges," Mason said, watching the guy gather everyone close. Sure enough he explained the history of sponge diving and how the small community had become "the sponge capital of the world." The man standing next to the diver went on to explain about how expert sponge divers had come from Greece, settling in Tarpon Springs, creating the entire industry that supported the town and which had become a major tourist attraction.

Mason and Gina watched with fascination along with several other people as the man went down into the water in the heavy suit, assisted by his friend, and came up moments later holding a wet, dark brown sponge that was covered with muck.

Making his way back over the rail, the rakish Greek diver allowed everyone to touch and explore the sponge, and in his accent explained what would happen to the raw sponges once they went back to dock and were cleaned and trimmed for sale. It was a practiced speech, obviously given over and over, but Mason also noted how genuinely the man appeared to love his work.

"They are wonderful," Gina said about the sponges. "It's all I've ever used, though I found them at the beauty shop. I'd been here before, when we were kids, but we never took the tour. It's interesting to see where they really come from."

Mason nodded, though his mind drifted off to a fantasy of washing Gina from top to toe with one of the soft sponges, working it over her smooth skin, leaving no spot unexplored. He put some money in the tip jar that was provided as they walked off the boat, and in the shop bought some of the sponges with the idea of making that fantasy a reality.

LATER, AFTER RETURNING HOME and changing clothes, they walked among the dinner crowd under the numerous Greek flags along the street, hand-in-hand, enjoying the Mediterranean atmosphere of the town. They appeared every bit the vacationing lovers as they strolled on their way to a romantic dinner.

Gina wore the gauzy goddess dress, loving how the soft, filmy material swished against her skin, leaving her legs exposed below the knee and her shoulders bare to catch the fresh breeze coming off of the water.

It was playacting, complete with new names, calling each other Roger and Annette in the presence of others. They perused some shops and walked through the dark halls of a somewhat homemade museum in the back of a store that illustrated the history of the area.

As Mason was caught up in conversation with one of the store's owners, Gina drifted away and looked through bins of cute souvenir items and absently picked through a bin of sponges. The day had been wonderful, but her mind went back to Tracy, and her mood took a nosedive.

Here she was, safe and sound, with Mason, while Tracy could be in some horrible situation. It wasn't right. But what could she do?

Her eye caught sight of a display of disposable cell phones, and peeping to see where Mason was, she quickly grabbed one and bought it, unwrapping it and stuffing it in her purse before Mason could see.

They couldn't be traced, at least that's what she'd heard. If she tried to call Tracy, who would know? What would it hurt? She hated sneaking behind Mason's back, but she needed to call Tracy, to at least try to make contact. There had been no word from the federal agents, and Gina couldn't just sit by and do nothing.

"Are you ready?" Mason asked, his eyes drifting over her in the dress appreciatively.

"Yes, I was just browsing," she said, smiling brightly as she kept her purse—and the phone—close at her side.

They left the store and the air had cooled considerably. Gina enjoyed the warmth of Mason's arm around her shoulders, and how he pulled her in closer as they walked. There were a number of Greek and Spanish restaurants to choose from, and she imagined all of them were probably wonderful. Everything around them was authentic, including the food. It made their pretense stand out for her, uncomfortably so.

"You look gorgeous in that dress, but I can't wait to get home and get it off of you, Annette," Mason whispered in her ear as he held open the door to one of the Greek restaurants with one hand, and guided her ahead of him with his other on the small of her back.

She looked back at him flirtatiously, batting her eyelashes. "You clean up pretty well yourself, Rog," she said on a purr, taking him by the lapel of his casual summer blazer and pulling him in for a quick kiss.

They turned to find the hostess—a lovely, older Greek woman with a wide, welcoming smile—watching them approvingly. She sat them at a lovely table near the window where Gina could equally enjoy the view of the quaint street and the adjoined bakery, where pastries and confections beckoned to her.

The dress made her feel like a princess, and the candle on the table flickered softly as the server brought them two glasses of wine that she hadn't even heard Mason order.

"To Roger and Annette," he said, lifting his glass, his eyes looking deeply into hers.

She lifted her glass, as well, tapping it to his. "While we live, let's live," she said softly.

"That's a nice sentiment," he said after a sip.

"My dad always said it, and it seemed apt," she replied, habit forcing her to test the wine carefully, finding it a tad tannic but still very nice for the price point. "Sort of like what you were saying about us taking the chance to enjoy this time, even in the situation."

Desire darkened the green in his eyes in the most intriguing way. And she couldn't deny it, she got a total rush from seeing his need for her reflected in his face. Could she tell him about the phone and her plan to call Tracy? Could she trust him? As she studied the menu, she barely saw the offerings listed there.

"What? What's the matter, Gina?" Mason asked.

She pushed her thoughts aside. "Living in the moment isn't always easy, I guess. I know there's nothing we can do, and I want to be with you, to enjoy what we can while we can, but reality…it's always hovering. How can I sit here, dressed up and having dinner, when who knows where my sister is…if she's even…"

Tears threatened, and Gina knew she'd been holding

it back, stuffing her worries and fears underneath the thin layer of make-believe, distracting herself with living out her fantasy so that she didn't go insane thinking the worst.

Yet she couldn't pretend forever. It just wasn't part of her nature. Her training as a journalist, even if she was only a restaurant reviewer, had made her a realist.

"Hey. Stop it," he said gently. "If they knew anything, they'd call us or let us know immediately."

Gina dabbed at her cheeks with a tissue from her purse, glad she never wore heavy makeup, but not wanting to draw any attention.

"I know, but—"

"No buts. She'll be okay, I promise."

"How can you do that? How can you know?"

"Because until we know otherwise, it's better to have faith, right? And you have nothing to feel guilty about. Tracy made her own bed here, and that's harsh, but it's also true. And as much as I don't like how we came to be here, I can't regret being here with you right now."

Wiping away the last of the tears, she smiled. "I'll try not to let it get to me. I know I'm being a baby."

"No. Not at all. But maybe I can help you refocus," he said, reaching down to capture her foot by the ankle and bringing it up to his lap where he stroked the tender bottom in a motion that should have tickled. Instead, it muddled her thoughts and suffused her with erotic heat just as the server came to take their order.

Thank goodness she ate out at restaurants for a

living, and Greek food was among her favorites. She tried to pull her foot back, but Mason didn't let go, continuing to stroke as she ordered in a voice that was husky. The server, a young Greek who let his handsome eyes linger on her for a moment longer than necessary, wrote down the order before he turned to Mason.

"Don't be embarrassed. The Greeks are passionate people and you're too sexy to stay unnoticed," he teased her, a sparkle in his eye. "But maybe I should worry. We're supposed to keep a low profile, and here you are, looking so beautiful, flirting with young waiters."

"Hey, you're the one playing footsie! You know my feet are…sensitive," she accused with a barely repressed smile, as she glanced toward the handsome young waiter. "He's a decade younger than me, anyway."

"He shows remarkable taste for his age."

Gina smiled, flustered, her sexy persona failing her under his sexy scrutiny. She wasn't used to being complimented this way. Men had always been attracted to Tracy, but Gina had never been a man-magnet, and said as much.

"Get used to it, hot stuff, because I'm just getting started."

His grin was devilish and irresistible, and she found it easy to become Annette again, just for a little while. Flirting and playacting helped set Gina's troubles aside. Another glass of wine helped, as well, she suggested, raising her glass.

"Tell me more about your family. You already know about some of mine. Tracy, anyway," she said.

"Well, there's my brother, Ryan. He's four years younger, my only sibling. We're pretty different, but we're still close. My parents were really good at helping us be friends and not letting us fall into unhealthy competition."

"Is he a lawyer, too?"

"No, he's a bartender," Mason said with a grin. "He's a great guy. He has his MBA, actually, but he really loves being on the beach, serving drinks, and it's just who he is. He surfs, goes on trips in the winter to Hawaii and other surfing destinations. He's always living in the moment. I admire that," Mason said.

"Wow. You two sound so different. Are your parents disappointed that he never used his business degree? You sound proud of him," she said, watching him closely. He shrugged.

"He's a good guy. Fun, reliable, smart. He knows what's right for him, and he goes after it. Why wouldn't we be proud of him?"

"I guess I figured you probably came from one of those high-powered families, you know, where everyone is a doctor or lawyer, that kind of thing."

"Nope. My parents always had a 'be who you are' attitude, and they never really pressured us in any particular direction."

"What do they do?"

"My mother is a high school teacher, and Dad owns a small computer software company now. He was a consultant for years, but the travel was wearing thin, so he started the company while we were in college. It's not a big player in the market, but it has a firm niche and does well enough to keep him happy with it."

"How did you get into law?"

"I like to argue," he said with a smile, winking at her and she laughed.

"Seriously."

"It was kind of like how you became a food critic, in a way. I started out as an English major, and I really liked writing, research and heavy-duty issue papers for my classes, got on the debate team, that kind of thing. One day I realized how many of my friends' parents had broken up, and mine had always been so close. I thought divorce law would be a good place to be. A chance to help people through a bad time in their lives. Maybe to even help them avoid it."

"That hardly sounds like what most people think about divorce lawyers. You help people *not* get a divorce?"

"Sometimes it works out that way. I can arbitrate, as well as take care of the split," he said, nodding. "But it's mostly trying to make it civilized and fair. To do the right thing."

She took a thoughtful bite of her entrée and looked at him closely. Mason was so positive in his outlook, a sensualist and a romantic. It intrigued her.

"How do you keep from getting jaded or cynical about things when you see people breaking up all the time?"

"I have good examples in my family, but I also see

people get back together, and while some divorces can be ugly, well, I just prefer to believe in love, I guess. It's a conscious choice."

"I don't imagine it's ever that easy."

"No, but having rules to work by does help, even if they are changing all the time, and the human element complicates things, of course. Sometimes I do feel awful when I see it all fall apart, especially when there are kids involved, but then I just try to help and make it as smooth as possible. How about your parents? Are they together?"

Gina shrugged. "Oh, yeah, they're very happy."

"You mentioned your dad is your stepparent. So you were a child of divorce?"

She smiled. "No, I was a child of a very good marriage between two people who loved each other, my mom has made sure I knew that, but then my dad died early. I barely remember, though I have some pictures."

"So your mom remarried?"

"Yes, and had Tracy."

"So you are half sisters."

"Yeah, but that's just the biology. We were never raised that way. Always just sisters."

"That's nice. Sorry you lost your dad so young, though."

"I don't remember too much. I wasn't even in kindergarten yet. I know my mother loved him, and she was lucky enough to find someone else she loved, too. I imagine that's rare."

Mason nodded. "A lot of people never even find one love in their life, let alone two."

Gina had never really thought of it in those terms before, but as they talked, and Mason told her some stories of the past divorces he had handled—no names, of course—her appreciation of what he did and what kind of man he was blossomed.

He obviously did well in his line of work, but he seemed truly dedicated to doing the right thing, not just taking advantage of people at a low point in their lives. All of the nasty lawyer jokes she had ever heard now rang hollow.

Some of his stories were funny, as well. He had her laughing, touched her heart, and did it all within the time of their dinner.

Dangerous.

In spite of his talk about wanting more or thinking what they had was special, she kept her eye on reality, which was only a phone call away. At any second, this fantasy could end, and end horribly, depending on what the FBI discovered.

She was smarter to keep a firm check on her emotions in the meanwhile. Maybe, if she could contact Tracy, and make sure she was okay, they could end this thing sooner than later, before Gina started letting herself fall for Mason Scott.

They left the restaurant, too full for dessert, but bringing bags filled with delicate pastries and goodies from the bakery along with them. Pulling into the drive, they spent several long, heated moments in the car kissing and Gina laughed against Mason's lips.

"I haven't made out in a car for many, many years," she said.

"Me, either. Let's see if I have any moves left," he said, bumping his elbow on the dash of the small car, and his head on the ceiling, sending them both into more gales of laughter until the laughing was replaced with sighs and murmurs of desire.

Mason eased Gina's seat all the way back and carefully pushed the fabric of her dress up, maneuvering his large form so that he could kiss her inner thigh. To her great delight, he proceeded to show her some things she wasn't sure were possible in a car. His expert touch and the intimate caress of his lips against the tender folds of her sex left her wordless and limp in pleasure.

When they finally got out, breathless and eager to get inside the house for more, Gina noticed that one of their bags of goodies was flattened by her seat back. She didn't care one bit. Mason was delicious enough.

How could life be so insane and so wonderful all at once?

TRACY TOOK A DEEP BREATH OF clean ocean air, standing on the balcony of the condo that Rio said belonged to a friend. Their plan was in motion. They'd called Peter, and as expected, he was insanely furious.

Rio told her not to worry. He had arranged for a boat,

and they'd be on it and gone in an hour. There was no way Peter would find them. He didn't even know she was with Rio, and still believed Tracy was acting on her own.

Tracy couldn't wait to be away, to put this all behind her, but she did like how protective Rio was being. It was kind of romantic, she supposed. Being with him again was wonderful. No one made her body, or her heart, sing like Rio.

Being with Rio had washed away the memory of Peter's touch completely, and Tracy regretted her affair more than she could say. With Rio, she felt new again, like they had a second chance. Tears sprang to her eyes, as gratitude welled inside of her.

"Hey, gorgeous," he whispered in her ear. "What are those tears for? We're fine, you and me, together."

"But he's looking for me. And he's angry. What if he wasn't kidding before? What if he went after Gina, or my family? I should call her. I should—"

"We can't. It's best to keep them out of it. I don't think Dupree will bother with them, especially not now that he knows what we have. I'll contact Mason when the time is right and tell him to stop the divorce proceedings. Right now, we have to go. Are you ready?"

"How long?" Tracy whispered, her heart squeezing painfully. She wished she had talked to Gina, and that she had been a better sister. She was always screwing up, and Gina had always been there for her. They had their differences, but they were sisters. "I don't think I can do this. There has to be another way."

"It's only for a while. Once we are safely away, we can call your lawyer, Fitzgerald, and tell him to open the package, tell him where Dupree is. They will arrest Dupree, and then we can return."

"Why can't we do that now?" Tracy said.

"We have to stay out of sight until they have him. I have to know you are safe," he said, wrapping his arms tightly around her. "We have both made mistakes, but now is the time to set it all right. Are you ready?" he asked again, his voice and his touch hypnotic.

"Yes. Let's go. The sooner we go, the sooner we get back and this is over with."

"You're amazing," Rio said, smiling, taking her hand and heading to the door.

When he opened it, however, his smiled faded. Two large men blocked their path, and one struck out, hitting Rio in the head hard, dropping him to the floor. Tracy opened her mouth to scream, but all sound was robbed from her as she saw Peter step out from behind the other two.

He was smiling, but it was an ugly smile that frightened her. How could she ever have thought him handsome, sexy? It made her ill.

"Let us go, Peter. Please. If anything happens to us, my lawyer will—"

Peter's finely shaped eyebrows rose and he grabbed her hard by the arm. "Your lawyer will what? I think we need to talk, Tracy, and you need to give me back what's mine. You'll come along quietly, if you don't want me to shoot him right now, do you understand?" he said, nodding toward Rio.

Tracy could only nod. She hadn't meant to tell him about Fitz, her lawyer, to whom they had mailed one of their copies of the notebook.

"Let's go back to my boat. Take him," Dupree said, ordering the other two men to grab Rio.

They did, slinging their arms around him as if they were carrying off a drunken friend. As they hit the lobby, Tracy thought of signaling for help, but the hard push of Peter's gun into her side made her think differently.

Hope deserted her as they got into the car, Rio being pushed in after her. Their plan had failed.

9

MASON COULDN'T REMEMBER THE last time he'd been with a woman where work didn't still circulate somewhere in the back of his mind, but when he was with Gina, his entire focus was on her. They'd had an almost magical evening, and now lay together, warm and satisfied.

"I wish there was something, anything, I could do," she said against his shoulder, frustration clear in her voice.

"It's admirable, how much you love your family, and how far you're willing to go for them. But you also have to think about you, and where to draw lines."

She was quiet, letting him stroke and caress away the tension, and so he was quiet, too, letting her think. Family was a touchy subject. He'd seen a lot of family issues and problems over the years, some solvable, some not. But people never appreciated being told how to feel or what to do about it. Some things you had to figure out on your own.

He could feel Gina struggling with the dilemma of how involved she should be with her sister, and while he wanted to help, ultimately only she could figure that out.

"Let's get some sleep. You'll feel better in the morning," he said.

"I don't think I can sleep. My mind just keeps spinning around, wondering if she's okay, where she is, what's coming next. I'm going to drive myself crazy."

"How about a drink, then?"

She looked at him, her pale skin luminous in the moonlight coming through the window. He lifted up and reached to cup the gentle curve of her shoulders. He hadn't anticipated it, and he would honor his promise of keeping things light, but he knew what he was experiencing wasn't just casual sex. He couldn't get enough of her.

She excited him beyond the telling of it, sparking his endurance and his arousal like no other woman ever had.

Buying the new, daring clothes had been a good choice, he thought, thinking of her in the goddess dress. Gina was a sexy woman, although she didn't believe it. Still, as beautiful as she was in the dress, he could equally imagine hanging around with her no matter what she chose to wear. He could see themselves spending every night, and waking up every morning together, just like they were now.

Whoa.

He shook his head, clearing his thoughts, way too far ahead of himself.

"There are other, better ways to work off anxiety," she said softly, pressing a kiss to his lips, her hands drifting downward to wrap around him.

"You're insatiable," he teased but felt desire spark nonetheless. The open emotion in her eyes pulled at his gut. He loved making love to Gina, but there was a point where he didn't want them having sex only as a distraction. He wanted more. But he had to be patient.

He'd do whatever it took to make this happen, however ill-advised, he realized, as he stroked the inside of her thighs in a lazy way. She responded by opening herself to him further, inviting a more intimate touch, which he was happy to provide.

He propped up on his side, watching her close her eyes, her face tense with the increased pleasure his swirling fingers created as they explored the sweet area between her legs, her body stretching and arching into his touch, completely uninhibited. He loved it that she didn't mind him watching as he brought her to the edge, drawing it out until she begged.

Gina was a woman who put so much before herself, who loved completely and without restraint. Watching her come apart in front of him was incredibly arousing. He rolled over, gently settling between those silken thighs and easing inside of her. He knew that this was what he could give her now. Worry was chased from her features as passion and pleasure replaced it. That was all he wanted.

Whatever emotion was building inside of him, it was unexpected and wonderful. Precarious, fragile and new. He had no idea what she was feeling. He could accept that she couldn't talk about that, for now. But not forever.

Mason thrust his cock deeper into her welcoming heat, watching her breasts thrust upward as she thrust back. They had the perfect sync of longtime lovers, in spite of their short time together.

He wondered, watching her, was this just sex, just mindless pleasure, a distraction from her troubles? For him it was becoming so much more.

He pulled back slightly so that he could find the aroused pearl of her clit and tease it as he watched himself moving in and out of her lovely body. They were connected as intimately as two people could be, and yet there was so much distance between them. So many questions.

He didn't like it, and strove to be closer, lowering and holding her, wrapping his arms completely around her as her legs encircled his waist. He took her mouth in a kiss that left no room for thought, no space between them. She kissed him back just as ravenously, stroking his back with her fingers, and he held on, loving her as long as he possibly could.

"Mason, I—I," she stuttered breathlessly, breaking the kiss as he wondered what she was about to say, though any more words were drowned in a moan of sheer ecstasy as he felt her inner muscles coil around him again, her entire body tense.

What had he hoped to hear?

"Again, Gina. Come for me again," he said with wicked intention, rocking against her, stroking her inside as he increased the pace of his movements. He grabbed a pillow from the top of the bed and pushed it smoothly under her bottom so that she was angled up in such a way as her entire sex met his every thrust.

Mason was lost as desperate need took over and their cries blended as they both blindly sought their climax, giving as much as they took, moving together in perfect rhythm. He gasped as she came, hard this time, her hands clawing his back, inciting his own feral pleasure as he thrust himself into a searing wave of release.

He didn't want it to end, this perfect connection, and continued to move against her even after the moment had passed. Her hands drifted gently up and down his back; she wanted it, too.

He lifted off of her and removed the pillow from beneath her slack form, pulling her up against him and tugging up the covers. *I love her,* he thought silently, knowing that was where his heart was leading him. Silently, he spoke the words.

It felt right, but he knew he couldn't share his feelings. He'd waited this long to find the right woman, to say those words to her, and he could wait a little longer, because there was too much in the way right now, and when he told her, he wanted it to be only about them.

And also because he knew Gina was worth waiting for.

GINA WAS AWAKE FOR HOURS trying to separate her tangled thoughts and emotions in the dark of the room, Mason's heavy, warm arm resting on her bare midriff.

She'd slept for about a half hour, sheer exhaustion catching up with her before a nightmare yanked her from sleep and left her lying there, fretting, until she wanted to scream.

Gina thought about the phone in her purse, conflicted. She'd get rid of it as soon as she talked to her sister, and maybe she'd even find out something useful, something that could help.

She looked back at the bed, watching Mason sleep. That was the problem. She was sneaking this behind his back, not telling him. What did that say about her, about them?

She pulled on an incredibly soft pair of crop pants that flared out wide around her legs and the tank top that Mason had bought her. She felt like a gypsy in the outfit, the sensual material swirling around her legs, but it was comfortable, as well. Also a perfect fit.

Mason seemed to know her extremely well. Maybe better than she did herself. She considered the outfit. Was this her? Or just how he saw her? It was getting hard to know the difference. He'd brought out hidden parts of her, but was it real? Did he only want the fantasy?

"Hey. What's up? You okay?" Mason asked. In the dark of the room, she could only see the outline of his gorgeous body pushed up on one elbow.

What should she say? If she told him, he'd never agree. Mason was a strictly-by-the-rules kind of guy, and she wasn't about to pull him any deeper into this than she had already.

If she didn't tell him…well, she had to choose between lying to her lover and trying to save her sister's life.

"No, nothing. I can't sleep," she said softly, hating the lie, but hoping she was convincing. "You go back to sleep. I'm going to go watch TV for a little while."

"You want company?"

"No, thanks. I sort of want to be alone for a little bit. To think, you know?"

"If you need me, just say so."

Bittersweet emotions washed over her. She did need him, or was coming to. Maybe far too much.

He was a good man. The solid, sexy kind of guy that didn't often come along in life. The way he'd made love to her tonight had been…incredible.

Was chemistry just that, just sex, or evidence of something else? Tracy and Rio had great chemistry, too. Tracy had told her more than Gina ever wanted to know about that. But look where they had ended up because Tracy was forever leaping without looking. But that was Tracy, not Gina.

Mason was always amazing in bed, but the last time, he'd been almost worshipping her body with his. When he'd slid so sweetly inside of her, his hands framing her face as they'd brought each other to the peak, she'd seen emotion in his eyes that reached far beyond lust.

Or was that only wishful thinking? Her own, private fantasy?

Yet she'd lied to him so easily.

In fact, everything between them was one big lie.

She'd lied to him from the very start, when they'd met and even now, their time together was a fantasy, the clothes, the sex…it was all make-believe. Even with their incredible chemistry, that wasn't something you could build a relationship on, she reminded herself.

Wasn't it? Who was the real Gina? The reclusive restaurant critic who'd only slept with a few unimpressive men in her entire adult life? Or the sultry seductress in leather skirts and halter tops performing stripteases and letting her lover go down on her in the front seat of a car?

Gina was beginning to lose track herself.

She cared about him. He'd been so good to her, how could she not? It was supposed to be sex. Fun that was never, by his own invitation, meant to last more than a night. A fantasy. Still, the way he'd looked at her tonight…

Stop.

Gina couldn't do this now. She had to focus. Her sister's life was on the line, she reminded herself, slipping out of the room and closing the door as she heard Mason's even breathing, evidence he'd fallen back asleep.

She turned on the television down in the living room, though she didn't turn on a light. Taking a deep breath, she activated the phone and dialed her sister's cell number. Someone answered almost immediately.

"Tracy? Tracy, where are you?" Gina's knees weakened as the thought that her sister was really okay brought her huge relief.

"No," a smooth, well-modulated male voice replied.

"Who is this?" she asked cautiously.

"You could say I am a *friend* of Tracy's," he answered with a short laugh that conveyed no warmth at all. "An intimate friend. Who is this?"

"Tracy's sister," Gina said calmly. "Is this Peter Dupree?"

"Tracy said you were the smart one. I hope that's true for their sake."

"*Their* sake?" Gina repeated, confused. "What do you mean? Who?"

He continued. "Your sister and her husband stole something from me that I want back. Still, she won't tell me where it is hidden. I have to give her credit, she's tougher than she looks. So here's the deal—you tell me where it is, I let her live. You give it to me, you walk away from this."

"I don't believe you. Tracy and Rio aren't even together."

"Apparently they have reconciled."

Gina was mute with surprise. He had to be lying, trying to trick her somehow. "I still don't believe you."

"That's a chance you have to take. Is it worth risking your sister's life? I want my notebook back."

"Wait—what? I thought you wanted the pictures?" Gina asked. What notebook?

"I have those, courtesy of my contacts in the FBI. But your sister took something else, something much more important. I want it back."

A cold chill gripped Gina. What had Tracy done

now? And was she really back together with Rio? "Let me talk to her. I have to know she's okay."

Dupree hesitated. "You're on speaker. You have one minute."

"Tracy? Tracy, are you okay?"

Her sister, when she replied, sounded like a mere wisp of the girl Gina knew, scaring her even more. "Gina?"

"I'm here, Tracy. Are you okay?"

"Not so much," her sister said, obviously being careful with Dupree right there.

"What is he talking about, what notebook?"

"His notes…I took it as insurance, so he wouldn't hurt us…. Not a great plan, I guess," her sister explained.

"Where is it?"

"We sent a copy to my lawyer and hid the original. Fitzgerald is in the hospital, Gina. They almost killed him getting the second copy from his office." Tracy sobbed, her control slipping. "He showed me pictures of what they did to him, because of me."

"Tracy, this is not your fault. Is what he said true? Is Rio there?"

"Yes. I called him, and he was trying to help me."

"Um, okay," Gina said, trying to wrap her mind around that new information.

"Just tell him, Tracy. Tell him where the book is. I can get it, if he promises not to hurt you. I won't hand it over if he does."

"He'll kill me, anyway, and you, too. H-he sh-shot

Rio." Tracy's voice strengthened, then broke. "There's no point. He's holding us hostage here in this old shack, like a pirate who wants his treasure," Tracy said. It was strange, and Gina wondered if Dupree had drugged her. "Don't let him have it, Gina, don't—"

"Enough," Dupree shouted, and Gina cried out when she heard a hard slap.

Then Dupree was back on the phone. "You find that book, and you call me when you have it. You have until this time tomorrow night. I have people in the FBI— I'll know if you contact them. Keep that in mind."

"Wait, I—"

The line went dead and Gina fought tears as she held on to the cell phone for dear life until she got control of herself. What would she do now? Tracy was alive, but for how long? How was she supposed to find that notebook when she was holed up here?

The room suddenly flooded with light, Mason walked down the stairs in his jeans, no shirt, looking sharp-eyed and concerned, if handsomely ruffled in his sleep. He watched her as she clutched the phone to her chest.

"What's going on?" he asked. Gina had no choice but to tell him, and she also knew it was going to change everything.

10

GINA JERKED IN SURPRISE, crossing her arms defensively, the phone flying from her fingers as she did so.

"I had to find out if Tracy was okay," she said stubbornly, avoiding Mason's eyes. That was harder when he descended the stairs, coming up and making her face him.

"Where did you get the phone?"

"At one of the shops, earlier. I didn't tell you because...I knew you wouldn't break the rules. You wouldn't let me call her against the FBI's orders."

His jaw was tense as he nodded shortly. "You're right. But now that you did, what did you find out?"

"She's alive. She's with Rio, and Dupree has them both. He answered her phone."

"You spoke to Dupree? You're sure?"

"Certain. He shot Rio, and he's threatening to kill Tracy if I don't get him what he wants."

Mason shook his head. "They shot Rio? Damn," he swore under his breath, and Gina saw the color leave his face, making the sharpness of his strong features even more stark.

"You have to tell Agent Kelly. If you call Tracy's phone again, make up some reason, maybe they can trace the call, find out where they—"

"No! He said no cops, no FBI. He has contacts, people inside. That's how he got the pictures."

More surprise registered on Mason's face. "Wait— he has the pictures? He said that?"

"Yes. Maybe that's why they rushed us here, and you said you had heard something about a leak…someone got the pictures for him."

"So if he has the photos, then what does he want?"

"Tracy apparently stole some kind of notebook with important information in it. She and Rio were trying to use it as blackmail, but it backfired."

Mason let out a low whistle. "That's playing some serious hardball. She really should have just taken that directly to the FBI."

"I know. I guess they were thinking that if they had something over Dupree's head, we would all be safe. They made copies, and they handed over the one they had, and Tracy's lawyer—"

"Fitz? John Fitzgerald?"

"Yes. They sent him a copy, and Dupree sent guys to get it, and they did a job on the lawyer, Fitz. He took pictures and showed them to Tracy, told her it was her fault," Gina said, fighting back tears. "He's in the hospital. I guess Dupree figured this would get the message across. Fitz probably never even saw what was in the envelope."

"Maybe the only reason he's still alive."

"Yes."

Mason sank to sit on the sofa, his head in his hands. "Fitz is a good guy. He and his wife just had a baby. I can't believe this," he said.

"Dupree is evil. He obviously has no value on any life but his own. But we can't tell anyone—he'll find out and then Tracy is dead, too, and he'll come after us. I have to find that book, and I have to give it to him."

"No. Kelly said the guy leaves no loose ends. He'll get what he wants, and he'll kill you both. The only option is telling the feds."

"No. You have to promise me you won't do that, Mason. Please."

"I don't know that I can make that promise, Gina. This is way out of our control."

"What would I tell them, anyway? I don't know where the thing is." Gina felt her eyes sting again, frustration causing her tears more than sadness. "The notebook could be anywhere. But he said if I don't find it, he's going to kill her and come after us. He gave me until tomorrow night," she reported in a shaking voice.

"He didn't tell you a drop spot?"

"No. He said he would when I call him with the book in hand."

Mason stared at her hard. "He might kill you, you know. You and Tracy, whether you have the thing or not," he said stiffly. "Are you willing to go that far for your sister, who got you in this mess in the first place?

Who's only used you to get herself out of the messes she gets into over and over again?"

Gina's back stiffened. "What else should I do? Just walk away? Let her die?"

"No," Mason said, pushing a hand through his hair. "I don't know. I just can't stand the thought of anything happening to you."

Gina believed him. She saw the fear in his eyes. That set her back for a minute. He was afraid for her.

He let out a heavy sigh. "I guess if it was Ryan in the same situation, I wouldn't want to take chances, either. But if you are determined to do this, there's no way I'm letting you do it alone."

She shook her head. "No way. My sister, my problem."

"You make your choices, Gina, and I make mine, too. If you are determined to do this, then it's safer for both of us to do it together. Rio is—was—my client, too. Let me help."

She started to object when she realized what was scaring her even more than Tracy's predicament. Gina was more than willing to risk her own life, but Mason's? Even so, she couldn't think of a single reason to argue with him. And if she didn't let him help, he most certainly would call the feds. Tracy would be dead for sure, then.

"Okay, but we're going to need a plan."

GUILT STABBED AT MASON as he stood over the stove, making them some eggs. He'd seen Gina slip the phone into her purse at the store, and he'd guessed why she bought it. He'd already alerted Kelly about the matter, but now he had a choice to make. Did he tell Kelly what he knew, or did he stick by Gina? If he told Kelly, and something happened to Tracy because of that, he'd lose Gina forever. But at least she'd be alive.

It was an impossible choice. How had things gotten so complicated so quickly? Mason had thought that Gina's call would lead to a dead end, no pun intended. He'd never expected that Dupree would have Tracy, or answer her phone. Kelly had thought the same. But what now?

If Mason had thought that Tracy would get caught by Dupree, or that he might get anywhere near Gina, he would have taken the phone and tossed it in the ocean the first chance he had.

He'd inadvertently put Gina in danger. If anything happened to her, how could he not feel responsible? The only way he could live with himself was to stay at her side and help her in any way he could, no matter what.

So that decision was made. He walked to the wall phone on the other side of the kitchen, picked it up and dialed nine—all that was needed to make contact.

He simply said, "Nothing came of the call. No new developments." He hung up and walked back to the stove just as Gina entered the kitchen.

"That smells so good. I don't know how I can be hungry, but I feel like I could eat the whole cow."

"Adrenaline will do that," he said casually, though his insides were in knots.

He brought plates piled with scrambled eggs and

toast to the table, glancing out the window. The sun wasn't up yet.

"So, have you come up with anything on where that book could be hidden?"

Gina dug in to her eggs, nodding.

"Something Tracy said does keep playing back for me. I thought maybe she was drugged or delirious, but she said something about being in a shack, and Dupree being like a pirate after his treasure."

Mason frowned. "That is weird. Do you think she was trying to tell you where she was?"

"Maybe, but I was thinking…my folks used to spend a lot of time out on Caledesi Island. It was a hangout for us when we were teenagers, too. We used to play this pirate king game we made up. We would hide things all over the island, and whoever found the most treasure won."

"Huh. That does sound like a good possibility," Mason said. "Smart of Tracy to give you a clue like that under the circumstances. Have to give her credit. Not everyone would be able to think that clearly under that kind of pressure."

Gina smiled. "Tracy was never stupid. She's impulsive, and she likes attention, but she was more like my mother, more social and flirty—she would just jump into anything, living life to its fullest. I think I took more after my father, at least from what my mother said." She took another, absent bite of her food, lost in thought, before she continued.

"He was more quiet, more reserved. I think they were attracted to each other for the contrast, opposites attract and all of that. I always liked thinking I took after him. My stepdad, who's wonderful, really, is the same as Mom and Tracy."

"What does he do?"

"He ran an extreme sports tour service. He used to partake in most of the activities, though now he mostly writes about it. Though he did get my mom to bungee jump last year."

"How about you?"

"Me? Jump off the side of a bridge? No thanks. I guess I kind of separated off after college, lived my own life. I love them, and I know they love me, but we're all very different. They go scuba diving for Christmas, and I would rather decorate the tree and make cookies."

Mason finished his eggs, and looked at her with admiration. "And yet here you are, ready to take on a killer who has your sister. I'd say that takes a lot more courage than jumping off a bridge attached to a safe cord."

"There's nothing safe about this situation, it's true," she admitted, sighing. "Anyway, I guess the first step would be heading to the island and hoping it pays off. If we can't find it there, then I don't know what to do. Maybe we would have to call in the FBI at that point," Gina said worriedly.

"It's not far. There's a ferry that goes out to the island, and we can catch a taxi there. If it looks like we're just taking a casual day trip, no one should suspect a thing."

Gina nodded. "I appreciate you sticking by me in this, Mason, but at any point, if you want out, I understand. I—I don't want you to get hurt."

Mason's heart stuttered a beat. There was something in her tone… Was there a chance that Gina felt the same way about him as he felt about her? He walked around behind her, rubbing his hands over her rigid shoulders. They would have to sort out their feelings later. They had to keep their wits about them right now.

"No way, I'm in this as far as you want to take it. I promise you that, Gina, okay? No more talk about bailing out, unless you change your mind. Like you said, if we can't find the book, we may have to clue Kelly in."

He was rewarded with a slight softening of her frame as she turned her head to run her lips over his knuckles where they rested on her shoulder.

"Thank you, Mason. In a way, I wish you weren't involved. I hate that this is messing up your life. On the other hand, I'm so grateful to you, and glad you'll be with me. It makes me feel safer than all the FBI agents in the world. I know I can trust you."

Mason wrapped his arms around her, not saying a word, emotions clogged in his chest. When this was done, when they were safe and Dupree was put away, he'd make sure she had no doubt that he wanted her to be his. From what she said of her family, it sounded like Gina had always felt the outsider, the odd man out. An introvert living among adventurers, and it had convinced her she wasn't as interesting as her family. He planned to convince her differently.

"It's too late to go back to bed, too early to leave. Want to take a shower, get under some hot water, try to relax?" he asked, leaning down to nibble the back of her neck.

"I do need something to distract me until we can go look for this book," she said, her voice hitching slightly.

A little while later, in the shower, where he washed her silken skin from head to toe, he tried to drive away the demons in her eyes with sparks of pleasure. When their bodies came together, rising and falling on the ebb and flow of passion, he didn't say anything more, but hoped she somehow knew that he was already utterly hers.

AS THEY CROSSED THE BLUE WATERS to the island where she'd spent so much time as a child, Gina felt separated from the rest of the human race buzzing around her. Others were fishing, enjoying the beautiful November day, and she was preparing to meet a killer. She just hoped they found the book.

There was one beach on the island that they had gone to regularly, and through a patch of woods, a cabin that had been used for shelter in storms or overnight camping. The island was a popular spot, and hosted a Ranger station and a marina, as well as some snack shops and picnic areas, though it was largely undeveloped otherwise.

The entire interior could be hiked in an hour or two,

so it shouldn't be hard for them to find where Tracy might have hidden the book. There was one shelter they had liked to play in, in particular. Gina hoped it was the right spot.

It was a weekday, so the ferry wasn't very crowded. They sat in their seats, Mason's arm around her protectively as they made their way across the water. The way he protected her, touched her so sweetly, it made her want to cry sometimes. It just added to the surreal feeling of it all. As if she had stepped into someone else's life for a while, full of adventure and passion, and her real self was just waiting on the sidelines for her to be finished. Mason said he wanted to see what could be between them when this was all over.

It was a tempting proposition, but what if all of their chemistry, and his interest in her, faded away? Could she take that? Her heart was blossoming for him, even as she tried to fight it. To find this was nothing but a fantasy would be pain she would rather live without.

"Almost there," Mason whispered in her ear, and in spite of their dire situation, a flash of need shimmered down the center of her body. Making love in the shower that morning had been a first for her. Most things with Mason were firsts, it seemed.

"If it's still there, it's just past those trees," she said, pointing.

"We'll know shortly. You okay?" Mason asked.

"Fine. I just want this over with."

"Amen."

A few minutes later they were at the ferry dock, and gray clouds blocked the sun, making Gina pull the hood of her light jacket up. It was still warm, but she shivered just the same as they stopped to buy bottles of water—advice from the Ranger greeting anyone who was hiking the island—and then set off on their search.

It was all on her, she realized. If she didn't find the notebook in the spot she'd remembered, she would have wasted all of this time for nothing. Was Mason right? Should they have called Agent Kelly and just had the number traced? Nerves tightened in her chest as they pressed on, doubts assailing her.

"It's going to be there," Mason said confidently, offering his hand as they made their way along the trail, then off through tall shrubs and over some sharp rocks poking up out of the sand and into the tree-shaded woods. Mangroves encroached to one side of where they walked, and Mason stepped carefully to make sure they were on solid ground.

"There," she said, spotting the shack and moving toward it, her feet instinctively remembering the paths of her childhood.

"But where? Where would she hide it?" Gina said, mostly to herself, regarding the rickety cabin.

"I can't believe they'd leave it out here, where it might be damaged by the elements. So…inside?"

"Makes sense."

They went inside the structure, and looked around at the few benches that were put there, but this was a place to ride out bad weather or spend an afternoon during a picnic. There weren't cupboards or closets, just one room with very few hiding spots.

"Maybe I was wrong," Gina said, shaking her head as she ran her hands along the walls and looked up, but there just wasn't anywhere to hide things here. Her instincts had been off.

"Wait," Mason said, grabbing a pocket knife from his coat. Gina had noticed he always carried it, and found it interesting. Her stepdad didn't leave the house without his Swiss Army knife, which had other tools attached. Apparently Mason was of the same mindset.

She watched as he walked across the room, stared at the floor and stopped. "Here. These boards have been messed with, see?" He pointed to ragged chips at the edges, and wedged his own knife into the space, pulling up.

Gina gasped when she saw the small brown notebook wrapped in the plastic bag.

"Mason, you did it! You found it!"

He opened it, skimming pages as she looked on. "This is incredible. A record of all of Dupree's transactions in the last fourteen months...he kept track of every detail."

"Seems risky to write down things like that," Gina offered.

"Yeah, well, all businesses have to keep records somehow, especially when the people you work with are likely to kill you, it's probably especially important," he said, looking through the entries. "What's this?"

He paged to the end where something was taped to the back of the notebook.

"It's a birth announcement," Gina remarked, unable to read the language of the text, but the format and the picture of the baby with the dates seemed clear enough. "This must be how he discovered his son. Where he was. It probably includes the name of the mother...yes, see here, Elena. It's how he knew."

"And it's also direct evidence linking him to her murder and taking the boy, among other crimes listed here. No wonder he's willing to do just about anything to get this."

"But he's also going to want to kill anyone who's seen it," Gina added morosely, her heart sinking. There was no way out of this. No good way. She looked up at Mason, her hand curling into the front of his coat. "What are we going to do?"

His hand cupped her chin as he planted a solid kiss on her lips, sliding the notebook inside of his jacket.

"I have some ideas. Tracy was right about one thing—this is very powerful leverage against Dupree. He isn't holding all of the cards as long as we have this."

"What do you mean?"

"Well, he's threatened to kill Tracy, but if he does, then what else does he have? There's nothing to stop us from bringing this to the feds—which we should do anyway, by the way. I fully plan to make a copy and mail it to Kelly before we go anywhere."

Gina didn't argue. That made sense. That way, even if the worst happened, Dupree would still go down, too.

"Honestly, right now, I think we're in the stronger bargaining position."

"It sure doesn't feel like it," she said as they made their way back to the ferry dock.

"That's because he's trying to play the fear card."

"He's very good at it."

"But I think we can exert some leverage of our own. Make him come to the book, with your sister, instead of making us come to him. It's a risk, but there's no way around it. It's the only play we have, really."

Gina nodded, seeing his point. "I hope he goes for it."

Mason stopped midstep, pulled her in close and hugged her hard. "Me, too. All we can do is our best."

When they started walking, Gina watched the man beside her and knew she was in love. He was steady, brave and he had been there for her every moment since this entire thing started, and he barely knew her or Tracy. She knew in her heart that she was falling in love with him, and was helpless to stop it. Regardless of their circumstances, there was nothing make-believe about it.

TRACY WOKE UP, HER LEGS NUMB from where she was crunched into the corner of the small berth, plastered up against Rio, who, to her great relief, was still breathing. His copper skin was pale and hot, and his eyes blurry as they fluttered open, looking down at her.

After the phone call from Gina, which had been what

Tracy had prayed for, Dupree had locked them both down in this stinking place in the bottom of the boat, leaving them in the cold, damp space.

Her teeth chattered as she tried to smile, pushing back Rio's hair from his face and holding back her own tears. Her foolishness had led to this. She had put herself and everyone she loved in danger. She just hoped to hell that Gina had given the information to the cops, to someone, and didn't try to come herself.

"Hey, handsome, you hanging in?" she asked Rio, trying to sound encouraging, though in truth he looked worse than ever.

His voice was faint, and tears escaped as he did speak, trying to offer a reassuring smile. "Not as bad as I thought," he said.

"Gina called here. She'll bring help. You have to hold on, okay? Just hold on, because I can't lose you again," Tracy begged, kissing his mouth and holding him close.

The shot had hit him in the side. The bleeding had stopped, but the bullet was lodged and she figured he had an infection from his fever. She had no idea how to help, or how long he had left. Every minute felt like centuries, waiting. There was a glimmer of sunlight through the crack in the door, so it was daytime, but she had no idea how long it had been since they'd talked with Gina.

"You stay with me, Rio, I mean it. I love you—don't give up on us now."

Rio nodded faintly, squeezing her hand before his eyes fluttered shut again and his grip loosened. Tracy pushed herself upward into a crouch, the room being only about three feet tall, and pounded on the door, though she didn't know what she expected to do if someone answered.

She could tell Peter to take her to the book, and she would get it for him, but only if he got Rio to a hospital. He would probably kill her, or worse, but Tracy had to do something. She pounded harder, yelling again.

She gasped as she saw the light coming through the crack darken for a second, footsteps outside. Fear gripped her, but looking at Rio, she took a deep breath, ready to bargain with Peter, to give him whatever he wanted if he would let Rio live.

But to her surprise, as the door lifted up, she didn't see Peter, though Ricki had his father's eyes.

"Ricki! What are you doing?" she asked, peeping up and looking around. No one else was there.

The boy pushed the door open fully, and peered down into the berth, regarding Rio solemnly. He held out his hand to Tracy, who shook her head.

"No, Ricki. No. Your father would hurt you if you help us. You must go," she said, shooing the young boy away.

He stood there stubbornly with his hand out, and Tracy didn't know what to do. If she went with him she could be endangering the boy. If she passed up this chance, she and Rio were dead. Still, he was just a child, and she suspected he had seen his own share of horrible things, considering who his father was.

She took him by the shoulders. "You go. You go

now, leave!" she ordered harshly, pushing him back, tears stinging her eyes.

Ricki frowned and then did as she asked, running away from the berth, though he left the doors open. Tracy pulled herself up and closed the doors, praying that Rio would be okay, and that no one would find out she was missing. If she could make her way to the cockpit, to the radio, she could call for help.

Stepping gingerly up the narrow staircase that brought her up to the first deck, she looked around, seeing no one. Weird. Then, she gasped as something touched her leg, and she nearly kicked out in panic, until she saw Ricki again.

This time, he had something in his hand, and pushed it toward her.

A marine radio. She and Gina had spent more than enough time on boats, and she grabbed the radio eagerly, pulling Ricki in for a tight hug and kissing his cheek soundly.

"Ricki, you are a wonder. Now go, hide. Don't let them know."

It appeared the boy spoke English, he just chose not to speak, but followed her direction, disappearing along the passageway and out of sight.

Tracy made her way to the deck, and tried to stay out of sight, sliding inside a doorway, but looking around, trying to get some kind of fix on their location.

"Mayday, Mayday…is someone out there?"

Tracy repeated the distress call, and finally, a voice

crackled back at her. "This is the U.S. Coast Guard. What is the nature of your emergency?"

"I've been kidnapped, my husband has been shot, we're being held on a boat, *Sudden Death*—it belongs to Peter Dupree," she said, remembering the yacht's name suddenly, her heart beating frantically in her chest.

"Ma'am, can you tell us anything about your position and how many assailants are on board?"

Tracy searched around the shoreline, looking for any clue she could. "No, all I can see are mangroves and beaches," she said, gulping for air. "Please, we need help. There are probably three or four guys on board, but I can't see them. I think my husband is dying," she said, her knees giving out as sobs took over.

"Ma'am? Ma'am, are you there? Do you know your husband's medical status?"

Tracy gasped as she heard large, heavy footsteps heading in her direction, her mind blanking. "He doesn't have much time. Someone is coming...I have to swim for it."

The man on the radio asked if she was in the water, obviously confused.

"I will be in a minute," she said, pushing forward and running for the stairs as the heavy footsteps closed in behind her, leaping for the rail.

MASON WALKED QUICKLY WITH Gina to the front of the ferry office, hoping they would find a cab, but as it turned out, he didn't have to worry about their transportation.

Special Agent Kelly, standing by his car and flanked by two other black SUVs, belonging to his backup, Mason presumed. Busted.

"Counselor, Ms. Thomas. We take it you had a successful search on the island?"

Gina looked from the agent to him, her shock showing in her pretty eyes. "How did they know? Mason, did you tell them? How could you?"

Mason shook his head. "I didn't. I did tell them about the phone, but—"

"But you lied about her making a call, and you lied about there being no new developments. I suggest you bring us up to speed, fast, or you'll both be arrested for obstruction. That could cost you your job, Counselor."

Gina stepped forward, grasping Kelly's arm, and Mason saw the other men take a slight step forward. Then, to his complete surprise, two more people, an older woman and a man, joined them, dressed as tourists. They had been on the boat, Mason realized.

"You've been watching us every step of the way," Mason said, grimacing.

"Yes. And we need whatever it is you found on that island. We thought perhaps you were foolish enough to try to track down Dupree, but since that wasn't it, what were you doing?"

"Agent Kelly, you can't do this! Dupree could be watching. He said he'd kill them if he knew that you were involved. He has someone on the inside, the same person who took the pictures, and—"

"We know all of this, Gina," Kelly said, removing her hand. "The agent that gave Dupree the photos is dead. Killed by Dupree himself, or one of his thugs, we assume."

"But there could be others, and he'll know."

"What did he talk to you about, Gina? Tell us, and we'll do whatever we can to help your sister, but we can't help if you don't let us."

"If you knew we were here, how come you don't know everything?" she asked belligerently.

"The cottage is only wired for video surveillance, not audio. We could see you on the phone, but we couldn't hear you. So, we followed. Beck and Hartman saw you go into the cabin and come out with something. We need to know what it is. Now."

Mason stepped forward, reaching into his jacket.

"Mason, no, you *can't*," Gina protested, but Mason knew that there was no way out of this.

"We have to, Gina. You can't help Tracy from jail."

He tried to ignore the pain of betrayal in her expression as he handed the booklet to Kelly, his own heart sinking. Maybe if things worked out, Gina would be able to forgive him, but he doubted it, the way she was looking at him now.

Kelly's eyebrows rose as he looked through the notebook. "And how did you find this?"

"Tracy and Rio stole it from Dupree, thinking it would be insurance. Instead, he got them, shot Rio, and he's holding Tracy somewhere. He told Gina if she found it and turned it over to him, then he wouldn't kill her sister."

Kelly looked incredulous. "No, he would kill *all* of you, and we wouldn't have this evidence, which is enough to put him away for a very long time."

"We planned to send you a copy, just in case," Mason told him. "And we also had a plan. If you listen to us for a minute, it might still work."

Agent Kelly crossed his arms over his chest. "I'm listening."

Mason told him about the plan to draw Dupree out, to make him bring Tracy to them in a public area where they could make a trade. All the while trying to ignore the daggers from Gina's stare. To his surprise, Agent Kelly nodded.

"That could actually work. But we'd use agents, send in a man and a woman posing as you—"

"No. Dupree probably knows what we look like— he would never fall for that," Gina blurted. "And we can't give him a copy of that book, it has to be the original. We only have six hours. There's no time. I have to do it. It has to be me."

Mason nodded. "She's right."

Agent Kelly scowled. "Okay. Let's get you back to the safe house. We'll call Dupree from there. We'll get you wired and prepped to go in. But if he doesn't agree, if he won't meet you, we're going to be tracing that call, and we're going to move in on him. We'll do what we can for Tracy and her husband, but we're not letting this guy slip away."

Mason squeezed Gina's shoulder and tried to offer

a comforting smile. She stepped away, letting his hand fall. *Ouch.*

Without a word, she followed the agent to the car and slipped in the backseat. She wouldn't even look at him, and Mason sighed. There was nothing he could do about it now.

_11_

BACK AT THE SAFE HOUSE IN Tarpon Springs, Gina sat on the sofa, feeling far too calm. She was about to call Dupree, the agents around her having set up their phone monitoring to trace the call.

"Are you okay?" Mason asked, detecting the slight quiver in her hand as she picked up the phone, four FBI agents standing by, watching carefully, saying nothing. She was so angry at him for telling them about the phone, for exposing Tracy to more risk, that she hadn't been able to deal with Mason yet. In spite of her obvious rebuff, he remained caring and at her side. It was…distracting.

"It's going to be fine," he reassured her.

"I hope you're right," was all she said to him, the most they'd spoken since she'd gotten off of the dock at the ferry. Maybe things would be fine, but could she trust him? She had sneaked the phone call, but he had ratted her out to the agents and let her believe no one knew. Without trust, how could they go forward?

"We're ready anytime you are." Agent Kelly motioned to her, breaking her train of thought.

She wasted no time calling Tracy's number. It picked up on the third ring.

"You have the notebook?" It was Dupree.

"Yes."

"So you did know where it was."

"I remembered."

"Right."

"It's quite interesting reading, actually. Especially the baby announcement at the back."

"Don't play with me, Gina."

The way he said her name made her cringe. "I'm not. It just hits me that this is a very valuable item. And if I bring it there, I know I'm probably dead, along with Tracy and Rio."

"I guess that's the chance you have to take."

"No, actually, I don't. Since you will kill us anyway, and as much as I love my sister, I'm not giving this to you unless I know we'll be safe, so you can meet me. In the town square, Tarpon Springs. You bring Tracy, healthy and sound, and we trade. In public."

Gina was quite sure that she could feel Dupree's rage right through the telephone. There was a long pause and for a split second, she wondered if Dupree had hung up.

"You're taking chances—"

"I'm not stupid," she said tersely, playing her role as a tough cookie dealing with an international criminal. Over her shoulder, she turned, seeing one of the other agents tap Agent Kelly on the shoulder, apparently with some kind of news. Finally, Dupree spoke.

"When?"

"Two hours."

"Fine."

That was it. He hung up, and she started shaking so hard that Mason had to take the phone from her ice-cold fingers.

"We just got a report from the Coast Guard," Kelly said, shaking his head in disbelief. "They said they got a distress call from a woman saying she was on Dupree's boat, and that her husband had been shot, and that she was going to, and I quote, swim for it."

Gina's hand went to her lips as she sucked in a breath. "Oh, my God, it's Tracy. It has to be Tracy," she said, giddy that her sister was alive and had somehow managed to make contact from the boat. "But swim for it—what does she mean?"

"She jumped off the boat," Mason said with a grin, barking out a laugh. "She escaped. Did they go to rescue her? Do they know where?"

"The Coast Guard didn't have any position on her, though, so their hands have been tied, but now that we traced the call, we're coordinating the search location."

"So Dupree was bluffing. He doesn't have Tracy at all," she said.

"He couldn't give up his bargaining chip on the call—that means he'll show up, probably intending to still get the book and kill you, counting on the fact that Tracy hasn't made any contact."

"Even if Dupree knew about the distress call, he

figures all's well, she didn't know where to send the Coast Guard," Mason reasoned aloud.

"Very likely. But we know now. He's desperate though, and he'll be looking to get out of the country fast. It makes him more dangerous."

"So do I still have to meet him?"

Agent Kelly shook his head no. "We'll be waiting at the square, and the Coast Guard is heading to the boat. We have him one way or the other."

Gina felt faint with relief, and didn't object when Mason hugged her tight.

"I can't believe this is almost over." She looked at Agent Kelly. "You said she told the Coast Guard that her husband was dying—not dead?"

"That's what they said."

"Oh, I hope that's true, for Rio's sake. I don't like the man, but I never wanted him to be killed."

Kelly nodded and turned to brief his agents, moving on to the next phase of their plan.

As they all dispersed, he leveled a warning gaze at Gina and Mason. "Stay put. I'm leaving a car outside with two guys. You don't leave this house until I call and clear you to go."

Mason nodded, answering for both of them. "Got it."

Chaos milled around them, and Gina just watched as the house emptied out as quickly as it had filled. Quiet settled upon them, sudden and stifling. She rubbed her arms, alone with Mason and feeling awkward with him for the first time.

"I hope Tracy is okay. She's a strong swimmer, but it depends on how far they were from shore," she said.

"I bet when the Coast Guard finds the boat, they'll find her, too, probably on one of the nearby beaches. Or maybe she's found help by now."

Gina nodded, the silence falling thick between them again.

"So now I guess we just wait."

"Yeah," Mason agreed, and then heaved a frustrated sigh, stood and paced in front of the sofa. "Listen, I can't take this tension. I know you're pissed, but like you said, these are extraordinary circumstances. You took the phone, and you didn't trust me enough to tell me about it. I thought it was the right thing to do, telling Kelly—I wanted to make sure you were safe. That's all."

Gina took that in, nodding. "I know, I don't like this, either, but what does that say about us? When the chips were down, we didn't trust each other, did we? That's because regardless of what's happened between us, we don't really know each other."

"Or we know each other all too well. You knew I wouldn't agree with you making that call, and I knew you were going to try to go off, half-cocked on your own after your sister. You two have more in common than you think," he said, hands in his pockets, looking out the window at the sedan parked in the drive.

"Excuse me?"

"You and Tracy. She may be more overt about it, but

you are just as likely to take off and do something crazy, especially when it comes to someone you love."

"I don't think—"

"I didn't say it was a bad thing, babe," he added with a half smile, deflating her objection. Could it be true? Was she more like Tracy than she thought?

"Maybe you have a point. I suppose I also tended to play it safe because Tracy was adventurous enough for both of us."

Mason sat down at her side, taking her hands in his. "But you are as much a wild woman inside, aren't you?" he said, teasing, but also serious.

Gina felt her cheeks warm. "I don't know. I thought I knew who I was, what I was, but now...everything has changed."

"Like what?"

She focused on the wonderful feel of his fingers rubbing over hers, how warm and strong he was.

"Like not knowing if I want to keep doing what I do for a living. I think I gave up on my dreams too easily. It's been in the back of my mind for a while, but I...I always..." She started to say something, but bit her lip, stopping.

"What? Tell me."

"I always had this crazy fantasy about being an investigative reporter. It's why I got into journalism in the first place, but I just never had the... I don't know what it is. I guess I thought it was more of a fantasy, not a reality. Not something I was really cut out for.

There was a job opening I was looking at, before this whole mess exploded. It's probably not open any longer, anyway…but if it was, I think maybe I should rethink it."

"I think you should, too. You should always go for what you want. We both know fantasies can come true," Mason said in a velvety voice, his gaze fastening on to hers and not letting go.

"Do they? I mean, fantasy by its very nature is fleeting. In real life, nothing is as exciting as we expect it to be."

Mason barked out a laugh, startling her.

"What?" she asked.

"Honey, while the events of the last few days have been crazy, they've certainly been real. I don't know if I could take this kind of reality on an everyday basis, but life is as exciting as you make it. You make your own luck, your own opportunities," he said, leaning in to kiss her neck.

Gina shivered under his touch. "You really believe that?"

"I do," he whispered against her ear. "For example, I want you more than I can say, and I promise you, I plan to go for it…." he promised sexily, biting the lobe of her ear, and Gina closed her eyes as her mind went blank.

"Really?"

His hands slid up her thigh. "Oh, yeah."

"Reality can be pretty boring," she cautioned, trying

to maintain some kind of control under his mischievous touch. "You've never seen me in jeans. Loose ones, with a ratty T-shirt," she warned, but didn't move away.

He smiled against her skin. "Would you be wearing a bra under that T-shirt? Could it be one of my T-shirts, maybe?"

"Sometimes," she said, a grin flitting around her lips. "Nothing puts you off, does it?"

"There is nothing you can say, do or wear that could turn me off, so you might as well get used to that fact," Mason said, pushing Gina back into the cushions of the sofa.

Her eyes shone with excitement, but her tone was serious. "Mason, there are federal agents outside, in the driveway."

"So, they aren't looking," he said, wedging a knee in between her thighs.

"They probably are doing exactly that," she said, pushing him away, but without any real effort as his lips claimed hers.

After long kisses that left her pliant and warm beneath him, he pushed back, looking down at her.

"So can I assume I have been forgiven?" he asked.

Her hand came up, pushing his hair away from his face, and he closed his eyes, enjoying the tenderness of her touch.

"Yes. I know you are a man who will always do what's right, or at least, what you believe is the right thing to do. I know I shouldn't have made that call, but—"

"But if you hadn't, things might not have worked out as well as they have. Dupree will be captured, the evidence found. It worked out just fine, thankfully," Mason said, dipping in for another kiss.

"I guess it did, though I'll be happier when I know Tracy is safe, and when we hear about Rio, too."

Remembering that his client might be somewhere, murdered, sobered Mason's mood. He'd been a little giddy with relief, with anticipation for the future, but it was too soon for that, just yet. And very likely, after their little stint the night before, Kelly probably *was* watching and listening to their activity within the house.

Anything more interesting than kisses would have to wait.

"I'm sure we'll hear soon," he said, pulling Gina into the secure circle of his arms.

"And in the meantime?" she asked, trailing a finger down his chest.

"We wait, and we hope."

She nodded, but then lifted her head up, kissed him quickly and stood. "I can't sit and let my mind wander, though. I have to keep busy. Kelly and his agents should be grabbing Dupree almost anytime now, and I can't just sit here and think. I'm going to make some dinner."

"Want help?"

"Let me cook for you for a change. You can read or take a nap, or whatever."

"Well, that's an offer I can't refuse. It's been a while

since a beautiful woman cooked for me," he said, grabbing a magazine from the nearby table and stretching out on the sofa.

"Prepare to be impressed," she taunted saucily, and walked to the kitchen.

"I've been impressed all along," Mason said to himself, smiling, and settling back to read.

UNFORTUNATELY, COOKING DIDN'T take Gina's mind off of what was happening with Agent Kelly, or wondering and worrying about Tracy, though it did give her an outlet for nervous energy.

Peeking into the living room, she saw Mason had fallen asleep with his magazine, and envied him his positive outlook, the confidence he always seemed to have that things would work out well. Gina peeled some apples, making a pretty fruit salad, and wondered when and why her own view on life had become so negative. Why did she always assume the worst, or that things wouldn't work out?

That was something worth trying to change, starting with being more hopeful and letting herself be happy about Mason's obvious interest in her. The real her, after they went back home. He said she should go for what she wanted. Maybe he was right.

After all, if she could sing on stage and try to take on international criminals, couldn't she find the courage to take a risk on love? And she thought she might love Mason…or could love him. Given the chance, and some time to believe what they had was real, she could love him very much.

Grabbing a fresh lemon from the fridge, she hummed to herself, willing her eyes not to travel to the clock, where time was ticking by far too slowly. What was going on with the FBI? Why was there no news yet?

Returning to the cutting board, Gina reached for her knife and found it missing. Frowning, she scanned the counter, and then froze as she heard movement close behind her. Instincts had her opening her mouth to scream, but before she could, she was hauled backward, a hand tight over her mouth. Her head swam, but she felt, and saw, the flash of the knife she had been using as it was held against her throat.

"Hello, beautiful. I was disappointed when you didn't keep our date," the man said, and Gina recognized his voice from the phone.

Peter Dupree.

Her vision blurred as she tried to gasp for air, tears stinging.

"Did you really think I wouldn't check the place out before I walked out into the middle of that square?" he hissed.

Gina moaned, from fear and from the loss of air, her vision darkening as she found herself pulled backward.

"No, no, no passing out," Dupree warned, loosening his grip and allowing her air as he half dragged, half walked her backward.

"You're coming with me, and no funny business. I

have a gun, and anyone, including your boyfriend, who gets in my way, is dead. Understand?"

Gina nodded again, feeling sick, hoping to death that Mason was still sleeping. Where were the agents from out front? Why hadn't they detected Dupree's presence?

Dupree pulled her out the back door of the cottage and finally released his grip, dropping the knife and sticking the cold butt of a gun in her back.

"Why are you doing this?" she said, walking slowly across the lawn, trying to stall. Someone had to come help soon, didn't they?

He kept close to the side of the house, where no one could see. Though it was also dusk and the nearest neighbor could never see them from this angle.

"Where do you plan to go? You can't get away with this," she added. "They have the book, and they're looking for you."

"I know that. I saw them, waiting for me—do you think I'm stupid? Walking into a setup?"

Gina's heart sank. If he hadn't shown up, did they even know he had come here? Were they all still in town, waiting?

"We'll see how much they want you back. I want my son, they want you. They don't give me Ricki back, you die. I leave the country. Very simple."

"What about your notebook?"

"Unfortunate, that, but it's life. Because of your nosy sister, I'll have to lie low for a while, change my identity again, but it won't be the first time."

Gina didn't say anything. What was there to say? They stood by the corner of the house, and she noticed there was no one in the car parked out front.

"What did you do to them?" she asked, her heart sinking.

"You don't want to know," he said threateningly as they walked toward the car. "Maybe I won't kill you, for a while, anyway. I'll need some company if I have to go underground. You'd do," he said in a lascivious way that made her shudder.

"I'd rather be dead."

"Yeah, well, we'll see how things work out."

He pulled her back, put his cheek close to hers, his partial beard scraping. "You never know, you might like to live on the wild side. Being with me would be more exciting than life with your boyfriend in there." Dupree chuckled, and motioned with the gun for her to open the door and get in the car.

Gina looked toward the house where Mason was, thinking of everything he offered her that she had been so doubtful about. Love, passion, hope.

Every single one of those emotions came back to her in glaring relief, and she knew she wanted nothing more than a chance with him. She straightened her back and resisted Dupree's attempts to push her forward.

"I'm not getting in this car. You'll have to shoot me, here, but there's no way in hell I'm going with you," she said in a shaking voice, lifting her chin.

"Get in the car, or I will shoot you, and put you there

myself." But he didn't shoot her, and looked around warily, keeping his voice down.

Gina forced a smile. "You can't shoot me. It would draw attention, and if I'm dead, then what leverage would you have? You'll never get Ricki back, and you shouldn't. No child belongs with a monster like you—"

Dupree lifted a hand as if to hit her, and she cringed, but then he wiped it over his face, looking desperately at the car, his only way to escape.

Gina realized he wasn't on solid ground and she pushed her defiance. "You should just let me go. Take the car and go."

Unfortunately, it didn't look promising as he lifted the gun toward her and said, "I don't think so. You'll be on the phone as soon as I'm out of here."

Gina flinched as a shot rang out and she ducked, covering her ears, and then opened her eyes. There had been a gunshot, but she was fine.

Dupree was on the ground, rolling on the lawn, holding his shoulder where there was an awful lot of blood. Gina stared in shock, and looked up to see Mason standing by the shrubs on the other side of the yard, a gun in his hand.

"Gina, get his gun!" Mason called, snapping her into the moment as she lunged for the ground, grabbing the gun just as Dupree did the same. He groaned loudly, swearing profusely as he went facedown on the lawn, holding his arm.

"I'm bleeding here," he said between gritted teeth, as Mason walked closer, never taking the gun off of Dupree.

"Not enough," Mason said, still watching Dupree closely, never lowering the gun. "Gina, call Kelly."

She nodded, but had barely taken a step when cars roared up the road, screeching to a stop in front of the cottage.

Gina looked at Mason. "I guess I don't need to call."

Agents surrounded them as Mason put down his gun, and they apprehended Dupree.

"Where did you get the gun?" Kelly asked him.

"Off one of the unconscious agents. I woke up and saw Dupree taking Gina along the side of the house. I managed to get out the front first. I thought I'd jump him as he came around the porch, but I didn't want to take a chance on Gina being shot. I spotted the agents at the side of the porch, and took the gun. I have a license, and I know how to shoot," Mason added.

Kelly let out a low whistle. "That much is obvious. Thanks for not killing him. I hope we're going to have lots of nice, long conversations with this guy," Kelly said, smiling widely and genuinely for the first time since Mason had met him. "We will need you to come in, though, make an official statement."

Mason started to answer, but Gina took Kelly by the arm, shaking off an EMT who tried to get her attention.

"Tracy? Did you find Tracy, and Rio?"

"Yes, I'm sorry. They've been airlifted by the Coast Guard to Tampa General. Both alive, though Rio is in critical condition. His wound went septic," Kelly explained, looking regretful. "They think they might have caught it in time, though. Tracy is fine, she's with him. Scraped and bruised, and a little dehydrated, but she's basically okay."

Gina brought her hand to her lips, choking back a sob of relief, gratitude and worry for Rio. "Can we go to them?"

"Soon. You have to be checked out yourself first, no arguments," he said, cutting off her objections. "And then someone will take you. Mason can come with us, meet you later."

"Can't I come in and make an official statement tomorrow?"

Kelly shook his head, grimacing. "It won't take long, but since you shot the guy with an agent's weapon, we have to deal with that first."

Mason nodded and reached for Gina's hand, pulling her in close as Kelly turned away, his attention on the situation going on behind him.

"You go to Rio and Tracy. Call me and let me know what's happening, and I'll be there as soon as I can, okay?"

Gina nodded, wanting desperately to go see her sister, but also finding it difficult to walk away from Mason.

"It will be okay, hon. I promise. Right as rain," he said with a smile and a light kiss to her lips, before they parted, led by agents in separate directions.

Gina felt light-headed, and vaguely answered the EMT's questions, as well as those of the agent standing with her, but she only felt better once they were in a car heading toward Tampa, closer to Tracy, but farther from Mason.

It was the first time she'd been away from him in four days. It seemed as if they'd been together so much longer, she thought, thinking about his comments on time feeling condensed. They had gone through more in four days than some people went through in a lifetime.

Traffic was light that evening as they sped along, the agent with her silent and focused. That was fine, as Gina didn't feel like talking. She saw the lights of Tampa in the distance, and knew she'd see her sister soon. Right now, that was all that mattered.

12

"I'M SO HAPPY FOR YOU GUYS," Gina said, lifting her glass in a toast to Tracy and Rio, who was home from the hospital and back on his feet. Tracy had made dinner—with Gina's help—in honor of the occasion.

The table was beautifully set, gorgeous flowers sitting in the middle and candles burning, providing a soft glow over the festivities. There was just one thing missing: Mason. His place at the table had been cleared when he'd called to tell them he couldn't make it.

"And congratulations to you on your new job!" Tracy added, taking another sip of champagne.

"Thanks. I'm excited, though it all happened kind of quickly."

"You're going to be an investigative reporter, like you always wanted. Way to take the bull by the horns, sis," Tracy said proudly.

Gina *was* proud of herself, and she was excited about the new position. A few days after everything had settled down, she'd seen the ad was still posted on the Internet, and applied. To her shock, she was called for an interview and asked to submit a portfolio. She didn't have much in the way of investigative experience, but her references were good and Agent Kelly put in a good word for her, as well.

"I'm sorry Mason couldn't make it," Tracy added, sighing, and closing her hand over Rio's.

"Me, too," Gina responded, looking down at the dress she'd bought for tonight, looking forward to the first real evening she'd spend with Mason since their ordeal. They'd bumped into each other once in Rio's hospital room, and had talked on the phone, caught a quick lunch, but they were both busy catching up with life. When he'd called, asking her to dinner, she was in Miami, meeting with the newspaper executives for the final interview for the job. When she got back, he was in the Bahamas, working out a family situation for Ricki Dupree. She and Mason had just kept missing each other.

Maybe it was fate sending her a message. She'd found the daring red dress, knowing Mason liked her to dress sexy. But that wasn't the only reason. She liked it, too, she discovered. Dressing this way made her feel more bold, more sassy. It also gave her something more in common with her sister. Though Tracy's tastes were different, it was fun shopping with her, and finding they had more in common than Gina ever imagined.

Rio broke her chain of thought, and she looked up from her plate.

"Gina, I hadn't had a chance to tell you, yet," Rio

interrupted, his eyes sincere, his hand still wrapped in Tracy's. "But I am so grateful for what you did, and I want to apologize, as well, for everything that happened."

He and Tracy did love each other, in spite of it all, and Gina believed that. If they were going to make it, though, they'd need the support of people who loved them. She wanted to make sure she helped however she could.

"Rio, you gave us a big scare. I'm so glad you're okay," she said warmly. "I'm happy you two are working things out."

"We are going to make it work," he said with passion and determination. "I love your sister, too, but I was careless with that love, and I won't ever be again. I am determined to be a good husband, and hopefully, in time, a good father, too," he said earnestly, his eyes switching to Tracy. "I hope we can be family."

Gina smiled and left her chair to offer hugs to them both. "We already are."

"Thank you," he said.

Family or not, Gina very suddenly felt like the third wheel, and it was clearly time to leave the lovebirds alone.

"Listen, I have to get home," she excused herself tactfully. "Since I'll be starting the new job next week, I have to finish up some of my freelance work, get things in order."

"You're sure?"

"Yes, but I'll call tomorrow. Thanks for a great dinner,"

Gina said heartily, trying not to let her disappointment and her hurt show that Mason had canceled. Tracy, who suddenly seemed to have become very perceptive, watched Gina closely and followed her to the door.

"Don't be so upset that he's not here. He's just busy. It doesn't mean anything. You two are clearly crazy about each other," Tracy insisted.

"I'm okay, Tracy. I thought we might have had something more, but it was a fantasy. That was all, I'm afraid," Gina said, shrugging.

Tracy walked her to the door. "Nonsense. I saw how he looked at you that day when we were all visiting Rio. He looked like he could swallow you whole."

Gina appreciated the support, but she really just wanted to go back to her house, put on comfortable clothes and move on. She'd had the fantasy with Mason, which was more than most people had and now she knew she could reach out and live her real life to the fullest.

She hugged Tracy good-night and walked to her car, but paused, looking back at the warmly lit windows of her sister's home. Now a very happy home, because Tracy had been willing to risk everything to be with the man she loved.

Standing in the cool night air, the silk of her dress floating around her thighs, Gina looked down at her new, killer shoes and remembered Mason saying that she should go after what she wanted. Make her own luck, her own opportunities.

She'd taken a few steps in that direction. A new job,

some new clothes. But those were just the window dressing. Had she really changed?

Yes. The dress was fine, but inside, she had changed. She'd sat on the sidelines for too long, wasted too much time. Why was she wasting more?

Hopping in her car, she headed toward Mason's house. He wasn't home; he'd left a message from the airport saying his plane wouldn't be in on time for dinner, but she was enterprising. She'd sneaked into his house once before, she could do it again.

MASON MIGHT HAVE DRESSED AS A vampire for his Halloween party, but as he grabbed his suitcase and headed up the walk to his home, he really did feel like the walking dead.

He'd shuttled so many times in the last week between Barbados and the Bahamas then back to Tampa that he was forgetting where he was. But now it was done.

Ricki was safe with one of his mother's sisters on the Grand Bahama, and Mason had worked with Agent Kelly and Child Protective Services to make sure the boy would be well cared for. As they searched through Dupree's assets and belongings, any legitimate funds would be court ordered into a trust for the boy, and child support paid to his aunt. Mason had seen to that. Dupree was never getting out of jail, so he was no threat, not anymore.

Now Mason could catch his breath, and get back to normal life. Closing the car door and turning to walk up the drive, he saw a car parked across the street.

Gina's car.

His heart beat madly. He'd thought of going to her house on the way home, but figured she'd still be at her sister's, and Mason was too tired to be a party crasher.

He saw the light on upstairs and smiled. They had some serious catching up to do. His exhaustion dropped away. Opening the door, he heard music playing somewhere in the house, and he followed it through the rooms. She'd lit candles, and he saw a chilled bottle of champagne sitting on the desk in his office. And her bra hanging over the back of the chair next to it.

"Gina?" he called, stepping into the room, but she wasn't there. He saw a note sitting on a pile of clothes.

It was a costume. The note simply said Put It On.

He looked at the getup. Black pants and shirt, a cape, hat and Zorro-like mask. Looking at the dress, he wondered what she was wearing. Or not.

So they were back to the start, reigniting the fantasy. He couldn't deny his excitement, the anticipation of whatever it was that she had planned. He donned the outfit quickly and then looked down, noticing how rose petals scattered on the floor formed a path. One he was supposed to follow, he presumed.

"Okay, I'll play," he said aloud to the room, following the path to the main room, where a silky red dress hung from a doorknob, showing him the way.

He opened the door to his great room, where they had had the party. It was pitch-black…until one light came on, just a single ceiling lamp positioned to throw a column of warm light, effectively highlighting Gina. She stood in a classic cabaret pose, still, until he said her name in a hushed tone. Then she began slowly unfolding and coming to life, turning to face him as the music grew louder.

He had no idea how she was doing it, but it was breathtaking. She was dressed in the same costume he'd seen her in that first night, and it turned him on just as much as it had then.

Opening those luscious brown eyes, she smiled and bent forward, displaying a generous amount of cleavage for him. His cock sprang to life, his blood sizzling in his veins.

"Stay right there, Zorro," she cautioned, smiling a wicked smile, and tapping her foot on the wood floor. "And enjoy the show."

She was perfect.

From the first lyric, he was mesmerized, just as he had been then. Maybe even more so now, because he knew the woman behind the song. In this case, "Love to Love You, Baby." Slow and sensuous, her body moved with the seductive grace he couldn't get enough of.

She made it halfway through the song when he couldn't take it any longer. They'd been apart for more than a week, and while he'd been busy with work, she'd always been in some part of his mind. Now she was here, just a few feet away, and in spite of her sexy command, he wasn't going to stay away for one more second.

"Hey, you're interrupting my song," she objected, laughing as he grabbed her around the waist and pulled her close for a long, hot kiss that could never go as deep as he needed to go, never take him as close as he wanted to be. That would take a lifetime.

When he released her, her hat had fallen off, the sexy sable curls he loved framed her face. Her lips were glossy with sexy red, most of which he'd kissed off, and there was a bit of glitter on her eyes.

She ran a foot up and down the back of his leg, and he pushed his fingers into the silk of her hair, kissing her again.

"I missed you like crazy," he said. "This is quite the welcome home." She was warm and soft and incredible....

And his.

She smiled lovingly. "I missed you, too. I know you've been busy, and I wanted to surprise you."

"You succeeded," he said into the silky slope of her neck, peeling away the skinny spaghetti strap of the outfit and planting kisses all along her shoulder and throat. He was gratified to see the pulse hammering at the base.

"We never really had our fantasy night—not the way we planned. I thought it was time," she said, her hand on his cheek as she kissed him back. "One more crazy night," she promised with a sexy smile.

Mason stopped. "One night?"

Gina looked at him, and now he could see confidence warring with the uncertainty in her eyes.

"The fantasy night we bargained on. Unless..." she said, sucking in a breath, letting the word hang between them. "Unless you want more."

AS THEIR EYES MET, DESIRE AND something dangerously like hope flooded Gina's heart. His tousled onyx hair made him even more roguish and appealing. She dropped her gaze lower to see that he was obviously as aroused as she was.

She held her breath, waiting for him to respond. What did he want? One night, one more time for them to explore the passion that they shared for those few days? Or maybe something else? Maybe something more? Either way, she needed to know, for them to make a choice, and not hang in limbo.

"I love you," he said hoarsely.

That flattened her.

She gaped, not having expected that bald declaration. The mask framed his focus on her, emphasizing his eyes and all of the emotions she saw there. His hands were on her shoulders, and he shook her lightly, out of her surprise.

"Did you hear me? I said love you, Gina. I know it in my heart as surely as I've known anything. I don't want one fantasy night. I want lots of them," he said, bestowing kisses on her forehead, eyelids and then lightly on her lips. His arms slid around, gathering her in until they were pressed together, fitting perfectly.

"You love me?" Gina could only repeat.

"Completely. Utterly. I knew it from the start, but there was so much going on. When I saw Dupree holding that gun on you…well, I knew that without you in my life, nothing would be right again."

"Oh," she murmured, caught between the sensations his hands and lips were creating, and the mind-blanking happiness his words had created.

He loved her.

Mason's chest rumbled lightly against her own and she looked up to see him chuckling.

"That's all you have to say?" he said incredulously. "Oh?"

She grinned back, the happiness and hope that she'd held back bursting forward. She'd taken a risk helping Tracy, and it had paid off. She'd taken another, going after the reporter job, and it had gone well, too.

Somehow, taking risks didn't seem all that scary anymore, especially when Mason was there by her side.

"I love you, too," she said passionately, staring into his gorgeous green eyes and knowing she wanted to look into those eyes every day for the rest of her life.

"Wow, you had me worried there," he said.

Then his mouth was on hers, his hands everywhere. They'd had four intense days together, and then nearly nine apart. Desperation followed their declarations, costumes being stripped, clothes in a puddle on the floor at their feet.

When Mason reached for his mask, she stopped him. "No, leave that on. It's hot," she said, smiling.

"Whatever my siren wants…" he replied, just as he did the first time they were together.

"I want you, always," she answered.

He bent down and she gasped in surprise when he lifted her off of her feet, holding her close, his mouth covering hers as they walked upstairs to his room.

When he put her down on the bed, his eyes caressing her everywhere, she held her hand out for him to join her.

"I love you," she said again, enjoying the freedom to say it, not having to hold back anymore. He let her draw him down on top of her, cradling him with her body, enjoying the way he covered her. "Whatever life brings, it will always be exciting because of you."

"Yes. I love the costumes, the playtime, but all I want is you. You're everything that I've ever wanted," he confessed, his eyes on her. "And more."

Passion flared, and words were done as hunger exploded between them, even hotter now. Mason ran his hands over all of her, settling down between her thighs. Their gazes locked in profound emotion as pleasure took on new aspects.

Gina had a feeling that she would always be discovering something new about life with Mason. How could she not? Just then, she knew what it meant to give herself, heart and soul, to someone. Love was the real adventure, after all.

Epilogue

JOSIE RACED INTO THE TAVERN, late, but excited. She rushed up to the table where her friends waited, spotting her as she approached.

"Last one to the table buys lunch," Marley teased, and Josie nodded, hugging them both.

"No problem. I've been up to my ears with Carol out on bed rest, and I was grabbing the mail before I closed up for lunch, and take a look at this letter someone sent."

Josie hung her coat on the back of her chair and handed a small card to Kendra, who opened the card and read out loud:

Dear Fantasies-4-You:
I originally ordered a ghost costume for Halloween, but received the sexy cabaret singer costume instead. I'm not writing to complain, but to thank you for your error.

Your lucky mistake has changed my life. In fact, wearing your costume helped me find the love of my life, and to find my true self. It taught me how to reach out and take what I want from life, to make my own adventure.

So, if you don't mind, I'm not returning the cabaret singer's costume because I'd like to purchase it. If you can charge my account for whatever it cost, just send me the receipt.

Thank you for changing my life!

Sincerely, Gina Thomas-Scott.

"Wow," was all the girls could say, and Josie found herself tearing up a little again as she heard the note read aloud. She'd been such a mess these past few weeks, handling so much at the store on her own, and so confused about what was going on with Tom, but to think that one of her mistakes had helped someone find happiness was mind-blowing.

"How cool was it that simply wearing a costume had changed this woman's life?" she asked, giving her order to the waitress as she looked out the window at the bustling Chicago sidewalk, busy even as cold, windy winter settled in.

"It's like a fairy tale," Marley agreed, resting her hand over her very pregnant belly. Marley had found the love of her life the year before and Kendra was dating a great guy. Only Josie was still single.

"So what's happening with Tom, the sexy delivery guy? Seeing him again?"

Josie's excitement over the letter deflated. "No, and he hasn't called."

"But you said he forgot your number."

"I know. But he should know the store's number, right? He could still have contacted me, if he wanted to."

"Well, maybe he's waiting until he sees you in person. I mean, that last clinch you two had sounded pretty sexy. He's definitely interested."

"Maybe. Or maybe he met someone more interesting since the last time he came by the store."

"When does he come back in?" Kendra asked.

"In a few days. He rotates the route with a few other guys, and it seems like he comes around every ten days or so."

"Well, if you are worried he's forgotten you, maybe you need to take a clue from this letter. Find a costume so you can be his fantasy—one he's not likely to forget."

Josie perked up. "You think? I was wearing the sexy cheerleader when he came in last time...."

"Try something more exotic...something that really is every man's fantasy," Marley suggested.

"A love slave!" Kendra shouted out, drawing several looks from close-by tables, and they all laughed.

"Seriously. What man is likely to forget an offer to be his love slave?"

"We do have a really sexy slave girl costume at the shop," Josie said, pondering.

"Well, wear it. Wait for him to come in, shut the door, flip the sign and make sure that he won't forget you the next time," Kendra said authoritatively. "You're gorgeous, Josie. You just have to learn to reach out and go for what you want—like the lady in this letter."

Josie nodded, thinking as she ate her lunch. Maybe Kendra was right. She just had to find the right fantasy. The one that Tom wouldn't be able to forget. The one that would have him begging for more.

* * * * *

*Don't miss the next DRESSED TO THRILL,
HOLD ON TO THE NIGHTS by Karen Foley
Available next month from Harlequin Blaze!*

Celebrate 60 years of pure reading pleasure with Harlequin®!

To commemorate the event, Silhouette Special Edition invites you to Ashley O'Ballivan's bed-and-breakfast in the small town of Stone Creek. The beautiful innkeeper will have her hands full caring for her old flame Jack McCall. He's on the run and recovering from a mysterious illness, but that won't stop him from trying to win Ashley back.

Enjoy an exclusive glimpse of Linda Lael Miller's
AT HOME IN STONE CREEK
Available in November 2009
from Silhouette Special Edition®

The helicopter swung abruptly sideways in a dizzying arch, setting Jack McCall's fever-ravaged brain spinning.

His friend's voice sounded tinny, coming through the earphones. "You belong in a hospital," he said. "Not some backwater bed-and-breakfast."

All Jack really knew about the virus raging through his system was that it wasn't contagious, and there was no known treatment for it besides a lot of rest and quiet. "I don't like hospitals," he responded, hoping he sounded like his normal self. "They're full of sick people."

Vince Griffin chuckled but it was a dry sound, rough at the edges. "What's in Stone Creek, Arizona?" he asked. "Besides a whole lot of nothin'?"

Ashley O'Ballivan was in Stone Creek, and she was a whole lot of somethin', but Jack had neither the strength nor the inclination to explain. After the way he'd ducked out six months before, he didn't expect a welcome, knew he didn't deserve one. But Ashley, being Ashley, would take him in whatever her misgivings.

He had to get to Ashley; he'd be all right.

He closed his eyes, letting the fever swallow him.

There was no telling how much time had passed when he became aware of the chopper blades slowing overhead. Dimly, he saw the private ambulance waiting on the airfield outside of Stone Creek; it seemed that twilight had descended.

Jack sighed with relief. His clothes felt clammy against his flesh. His teeth began to chatter as two figures unloaded a gurney from the back of the ambulance and waited for the blades to stop.

"Great," Vince remarked, unsnapping his seat belt. "Those two look like volunteers, not real EMTs."

The chopper bounced sickeningly on its runners, and Vince, with a shake of his head, pushed open his door and jumped to the ground, head down.

Jack waited, wondering if he'd be able to stand on his own. After fumbling unsuccessfully with the buckle on his seat belt, he decided not.

When it was safe the EMTs approached, following Vince, who opened Jack's door.

His old friend Tanner Quinn stepped around Vince, his grin not quite reaching his eyes.

"You look like hell warmed over," he told Jack cheerfully.

"Since when are you an EMT?" Jack retorted.

Tanner reached in, wedged a shoulder under Jack's right arm and hauled him out of the chopper. His knees immediately buckled, and Vince stepped up, supporting him on the other side.

"In a place like Stone Creek," Tanner replied, "everybody helps out."

They reached the wheeled gurney, and Jack found himself on his back.

Tanner and the second man strapped him down, a process that brought back a few bad memories.

"Is there even a hospital in this place?" Vince asked irritably from somewhere in the night.

"There's a pretty good clinic over in Indian Rock," Tanner answered easily, "and it isn't far to Flagstaff." He paused to help his buddy hoist Jack and the gurney into the back of the ambulance. "You're in good hands, Jack. My wife is the best veterinarian in the state."

Jack laughed raggedly at that.

Vince muttered a curse.

Tanner climbed into the back beside him, perched on some kind of fold-down seat. The other man shut the doors.

"You in any pain?" Tanner said as his partner climbed into the driver's seat and started the engine.

"No." Jack looked up at his oldest and closest friend and wished he'd listened to Vince. Ever since he'd come down with the virus—a week after snatching a five-year-old girl back from her non-custodial parent, a small-time Colombian drug dealer—he hadn't been able to think about anyone or anything but Ashley. When he *could* think, anyway.

Now, in one of the first clearheaded moments he'd experienced since checking himself out of Bethesda the day before, he realized he might be making a major mistake. Not by facing Ashley—he owed her that much and a lot more. No, he could be putting her in danger, putting Tanner and his daughter and his pregnant wife in danger, too.

"I shouldn't have come here," he said, keeping his voice low.

Tanner shook his head, his jaw clamped down hard as though he was irritated by Jack's statement.

"This is where you belong," Tanner insisted. "If you'd had sense enough to know that six months ago, old buddy, when you bailed on Ashley without so much as a fare-thee-well, you wouldn't be in this mess."

Ashley. The name had run through his mind a million times in those six months, but hearing somebody say it out loud was like having a fist close around his insides and squeeze hard.

Jack couldn't speak.

Tanner didn't press for further conversation.

The ambulance bumped over country roads, finally hitting smooth blacktop.

"Here we are," Tanner said. "Ashley's place."

* * * * *

Will Jack be able to patch things up with Ashley,
or will his past put the woman he loves
in harm's way?
Find out in
AT HOME IN STONE CREEK
by Linda Lael Miller
Available November 2009
from Silhouette Special Edition®

This November,
Silhouette Special Edition®
brings you

NEW YORK TIMES
BESTSELLING AUTHOR

LINDA LAEL
MILLER

At Home in
Stone Creek

Available in November
wherever books are sold.

SSELLM60BPA

Silhouette Desire

**FROM *NEW YORK TIMES*
BESTSELLING AUTHOR**

DIANA
PALMER

THE
MAVERICK

A BRAND-NEW
LONG, TALL
TEXAN STORY

Silhouette®

nocturne™

TIME RAIDERS
THE PROTECTOR

by *USA TODAY* bestselling author
MERLINE LOVELACE

Former USAF officer Cassandra Jones's unique psychic skills come in handy, as she has been selected to join the elite Time Raiders squad. Her first mission is to travel back to seventh-century China to locate the final piece of a missing bronze medallion. Major Max Brody is assigned to accompany her, and soon Cassandra and Max have to fight their growing attraction to each other while the mission suddenly turns deadly....

*Available November
wherever books are sold.*

www.silhouettenocturne.com
www.paranormalromanceblog.com

SN61802

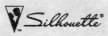

REQUEST YOUR FREE BOOKS!

2 FREE NOVELS PLUS 2 FREE GIFTS!

HARLEQUIN®

Blaze™

Red-hot reads!

COMING NEXT MONTH
Available October 27, 2009

#501 MORE BLAZING BEDTIME STORIES Julie Leto and Leslie Kelly
Encounters
Fairy tales have never been so hot! Let bestselling authors Julie Leto and
Leslie Kelly tell you a bedtime story that will inspire you to do anything but sleep!

#502 POWER PLAY Nancy Warren
Forbidden Fantasies
Forced to share a hotel room one night with a sexy hockey-playing cop,
Emily Saunders must keep her hands to herself. Not easy for a massage
therapist who's just *itching* to touch Jonah Betts's gorgeous muscles. But all
bets are off when he suddenly makes a play for her!

#503 HOT SPELL Michelle Rowen
The Wrong Bed
As a modern-day ghost buster, Amanda LeGrange is used to dealing with the
unexplained. But when an ancient spell causes her to fall into bed with her sexy
enemy, she's definitely flustered. Especially since he's made it clear he likes her
hands on him when they're out of bed, as well....

#504 HOLD ON TO THE NIGHTS Karen Foley
Dressed to Thrill
Hollywood's hottest heartthrob, Graeme Hamilton, is often called the world's
sexiest bachelor. Only Lara Whitfield knows the truth. Sure, Graeme's sexy
enough.... But he's very much married—to her!

#505 *SEALED* AND DELIVERED Jill Monroe
Uniformly Hot!
Great bod—check. Firm, kissable lips—check. Military man—check.
Hailey Sutherland has found *the* guy to share some sexy moments with. In
charge of SEAL training, Nate Peterson's not shocked by much, but he is by
Hailey's attitude. He just hopes the gorgeous woman can handle as much
attitude in the bedroom....

#506 ZERO CONTROL Lori Wilde
Though Roxanne Stanley put the *girl* in girl-next-door, she *wants*
Dougal Lockhart. Now! What she doesn't know: the hottie security expert is
undercover at the sensual fantasy resort to expose a criminal, but it may be her
own secret that gets exposed....